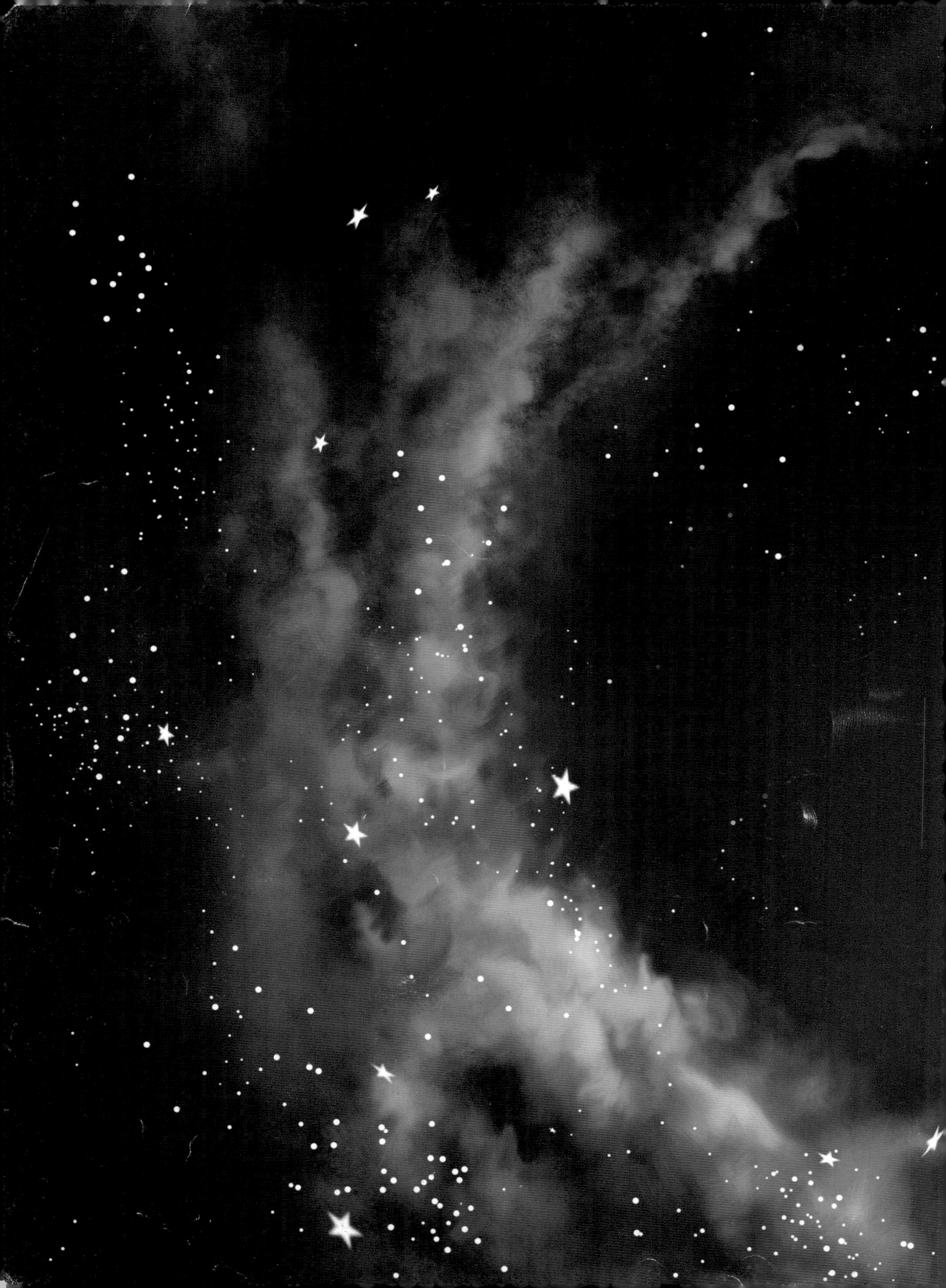

My dear Rose,

As I leave the Planet of Bamalias, I am still shaken by the events orchestrated there by the devious Snake. He persuaded a young woman to erase the painful memories of her past, and as a result, I lost all my precious memories of you!

With Fox's help, we were both able to recover our memories, and an entire constellation of planets was saved from disaster! But the Snake almost succeeded in separating us, and I still tremble when I realize that I almost lost you forever!

I can scarcely imagine a universe without you, my dear Rose, and all my efforts would be in vain if I could not keep you safe.

The Little Prince

First American edition published in 2015 by Graphic Universe™.

Le Petit Prince®

based on the masterpiece by Antoine de Saint-Exupéry

© 2015 LPPM
An animated series based on the novel *Le Petit Prince* by Antoine de Saint-Exupéry
Developed for television by Matthieu Delaporte, Alexandre de la Patellière, and Bertrand Gatignol
Directed by Pierre-Alain Chartier

© 2015 ÉDITIONS GLÉNAT
Copyright © 2015 by Lerner Publishing Group, Inc., for the current edition

Graphic Universe™
A division of Lerner Publishing Group, Inc.
241 First Avenue North
Minneapolis, MN 55401 USA

For reading levels and more information, look up this title at www.lernerbooks.com.

Library of Congress Cataloging-in-Publication Data

Bruneau, Clotilde.
    [Planète du Serpent. English]
    The planet of the snake / story by Julien Magnat ; design and illustrations by Nautilus Studio ; adaptation by Clotilde Bruneau ; translation: Anne Collins Smith and Owen Smith. — First American ed.
        pages cm — (The Little Prince ; book 24)
    ISBN 978-0-7613-8775-6 (lb : alk. paper) — ISBN 978-1-4677-6027-0 (pb : alk. paper) —
ISBN 978-1-4677-6199-4 (eb pdf)
    1. Graphic novels. I. Magnat, Julien. II. Smith, Anne Collins, translator. III. Smith, Owen (Owen M.), translator. IV. Saint-Exupéry, Antoine de, 1900-1944. Petit prince. V. Nautilus Studio. VI. Petit Prince (Television program) VII. Title.
PZ7.7.B8Plv 2015
741.5'944—dc23   2015001878

Manufactured in the United States of America
1 — DP — 7/15/15

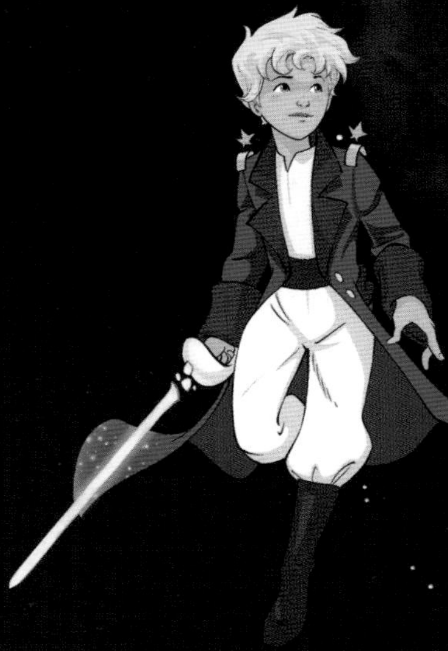

THE NEW ADVENTURES
BASED ON THE MASTERPIECE BY ANTOINE DE SAINT-EXUPÉRY

The Little Prince

THE PLANET OF THE SNAKE

Based on the animated series and an original story by Julien Magnat

Design: Nautilus Studio
Story: Clotilde Bruneau
Artistic Direction: Didier Poli
Art: Audrey Bussi
Backgrounds: Isa Python
Coloring: Moonsun
Editing: Christine Chatal
Editorial Consultant: Didier Convard

Translation: Anne and Owen Smith

Graphic Universe™ • Minneapolis

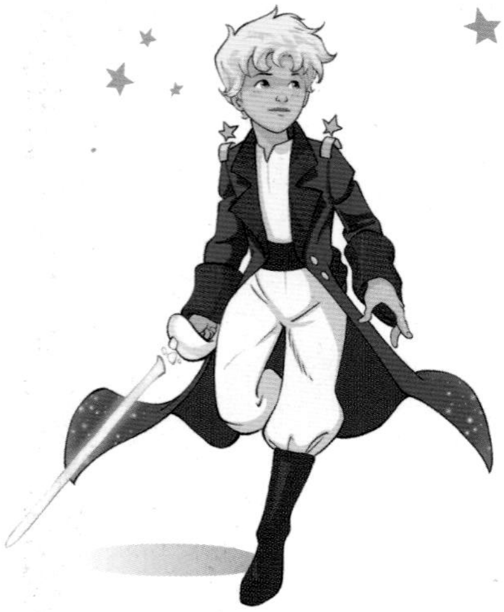

THE LITTLE PRINCE

The Little Prince has extraordinary gifts. His sense of wonder allows him to discover what no one else can see. The Little Prince can communicate with all the beings in the universe, even the animals and plants. His powers grow over the course of his adventures.

The Prince's uniform:
When he transforms into the uniform of a prince, he is more agile and quick. When faced with difficult situations, the Little Prince also uses a sword that lets him sketch and bring to life anything from his imagination.

His sketchbook:
When he is not in his Prince's clothing, the Little Prince carries a sketchbook. When he blows on the pages, they take wing and form objects that he'll find very useful. Like his sword, it's powered by stardust collected on his travels.

FOX

A grouch, a trickster, and, so he says, interested only in his next meal, Fox is in reality the Little Prince's best friend. As such, he is always there to give him help but also just as much to help him to grow and to learn about the world.

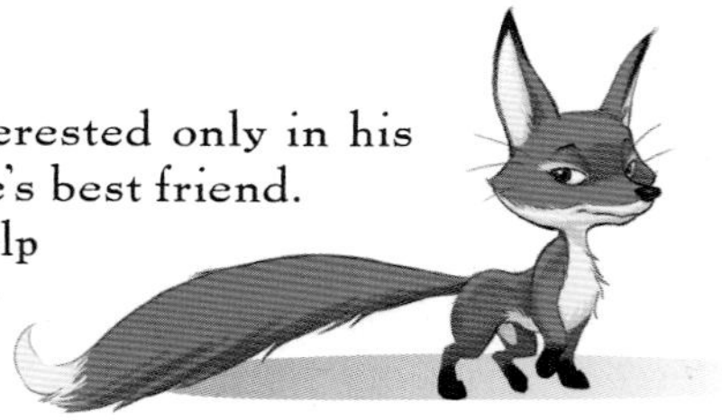

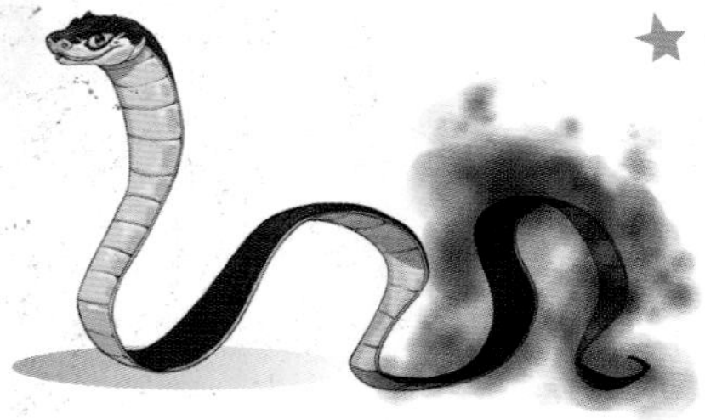

THE SNAKE

Even though the Little Prince still does not know exactly why, there can be no doubt that the Snake has set his mind to plunging the entire universe into darkness! And to accomplish his goal, this malicious being is ready to use any form of deception. However, the Snake never takes action himself. He prefers to bring out the wickedness in those beings he has chosen to bite, tempting them to put their own worlds in danger.

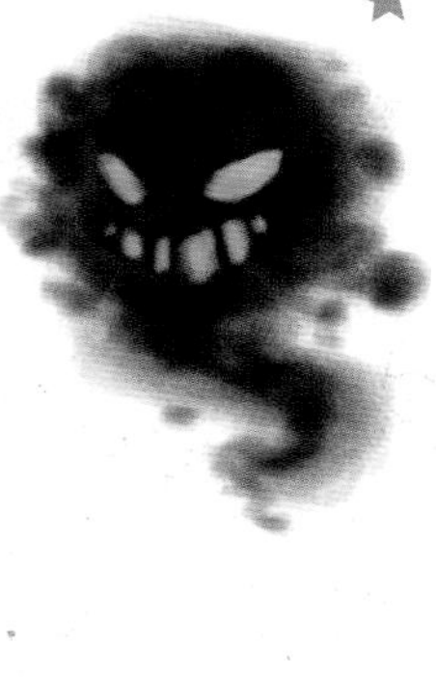

THE GLOOMIES

When people who have been "bitten" by the Snake have completely destroyed their own planets, they become Gloomies, slaves to their Snake master. The Gloomies act as a group and carry out the Snake's most vile orders so he can get the better of the Little Prince!

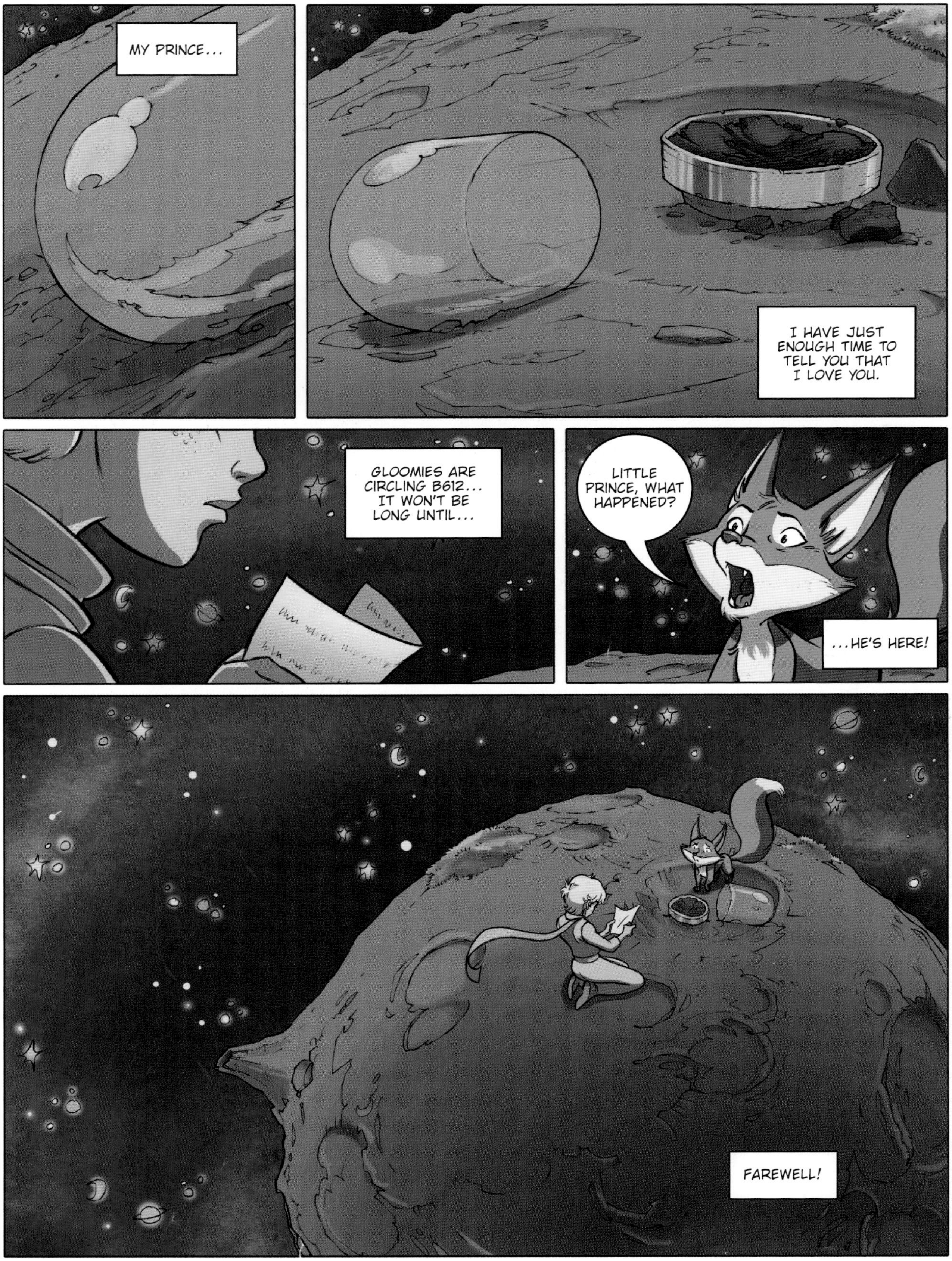
MY PRINCE...
I HAVE JUST ENOUGH TIME TO TELL YOU THAT I LOVE YOU.
GLOOMIES ARE CIRCLING B612... IT WON'T BE LONG UNTIL...
LITTLE PRINCE, WHAT HAPPENED?
...HE'S HERE!
FAREWELL!

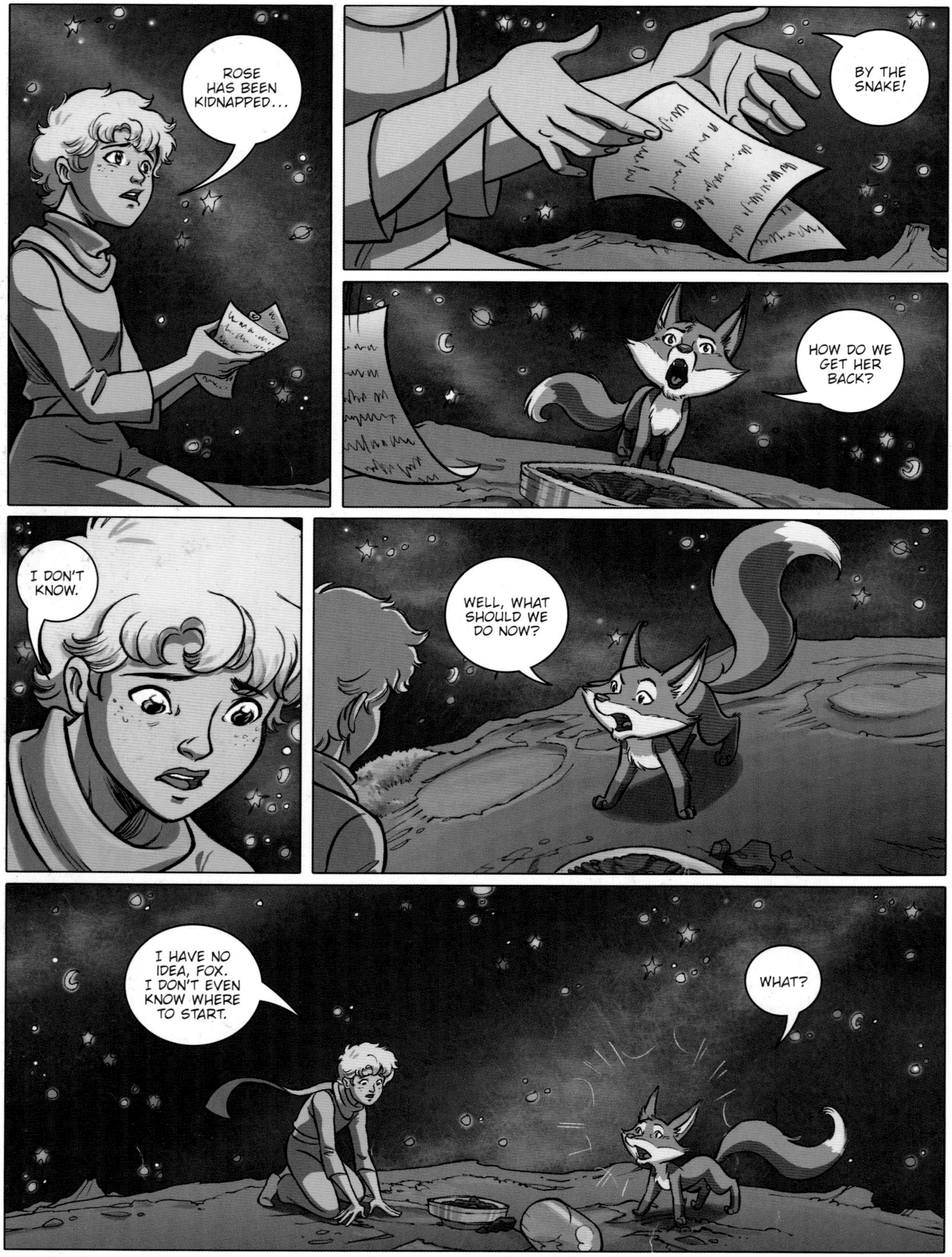
ROSE HAS BEEN KIDNAPPED...
BY THE SNAKE!
HOW DO WE GET HER BACK?
I DON'T KNOW.
WELL, WHAT SHOULD WE DO NOW?
I HAVE NO IDEA, FOX. I DON'T EVEN KNOW WHERE TO START.
WHAT?

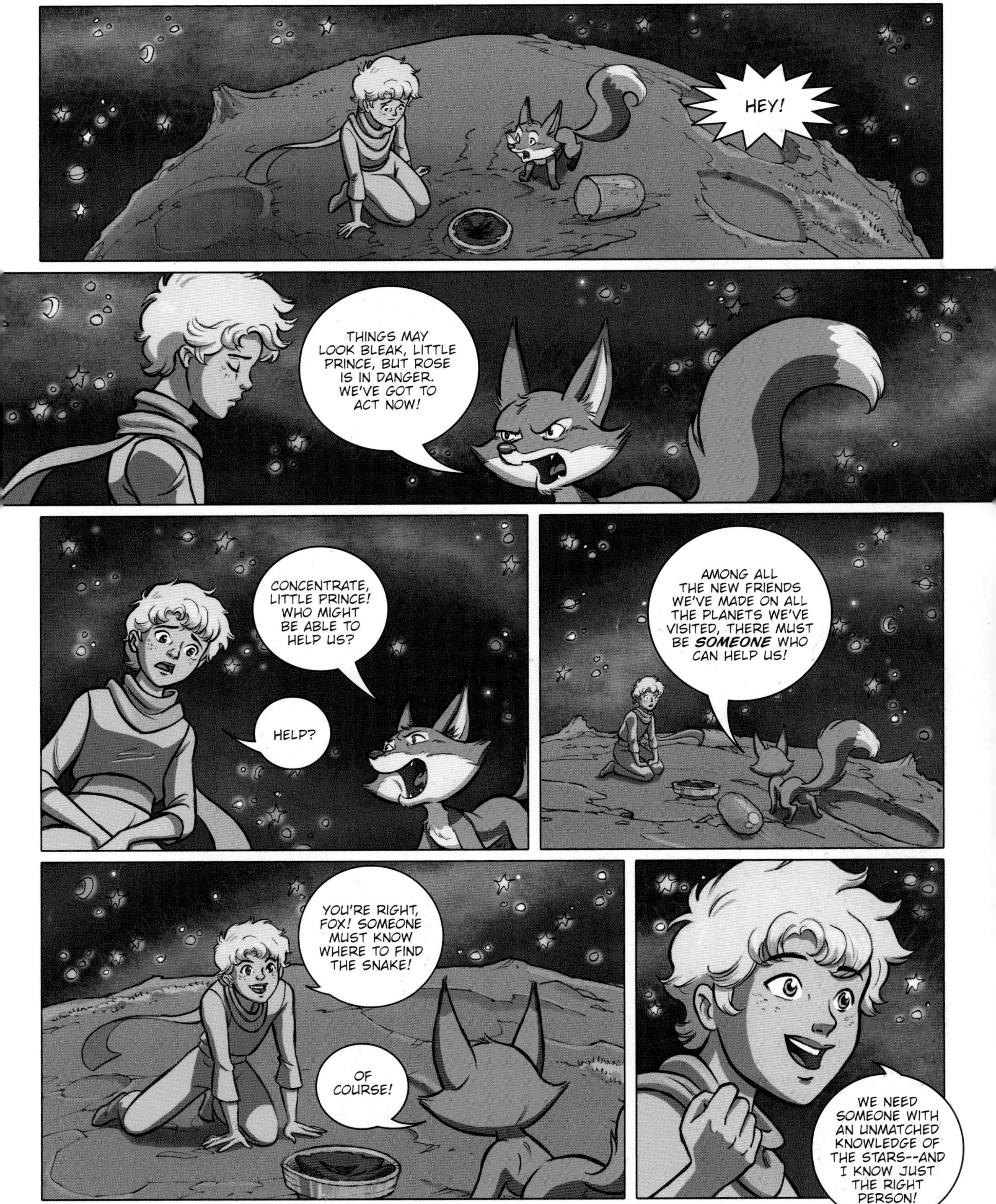
HEY!
THINGS MAY LOOK BLEAK, LITTLE PRINCE, BUT ROSE IS IN DANGER. WE'VE GOT TO ACT NOW!
CONCENTRATE, LITTLE PRINCE! WHO MIGHT BE ABLE TO HELP US?
HELP?
AMONG ALL THE NEW FRIENDS WE'VE MADE ON ALL THE PLANETS WE'VE VISITED, THERE MUST BE SOMEONE WHO CAN HELP US!
YOU'RE RIGHT, FOX! SOMEONE MUST KNOW WHERE TO FIND THE SNAKE!
OF COURSE!
WE NEED SOMEONE WITH AN UNMATCHED KNOWLEDGE OF THE STARS--AND I KNOW JUST THE RIGHT PERSON!

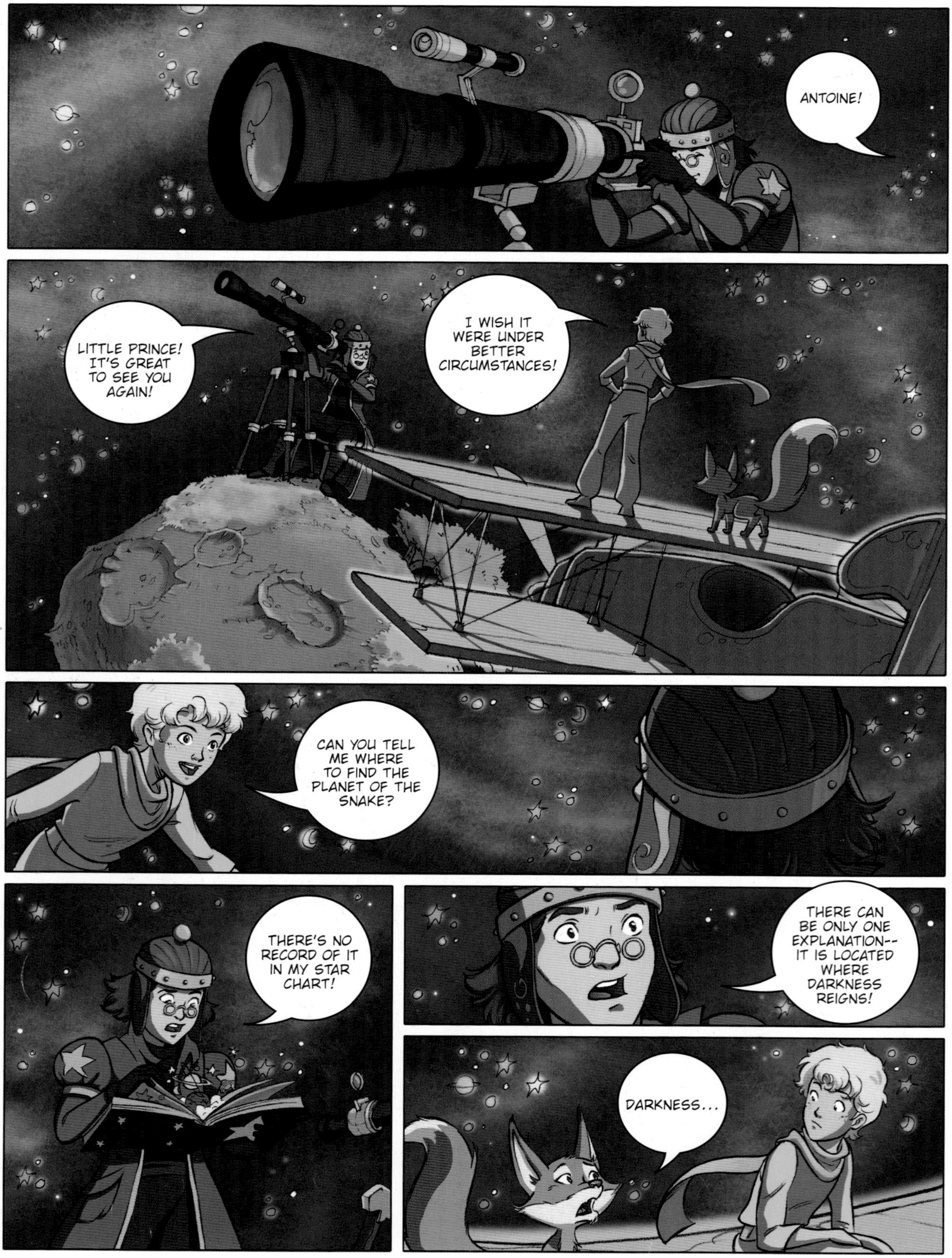
ANTOINE!
LITTLE PRINCE! IT'S GREAT TO SEE YOU AGAIN!
I WISH IT WERE UNDER BETTER CIRCUMSTANCES!
CAN YOU TELL ME WHERE TO FIND THE PLANET OF THE SNAKE?
THERE'S NO RECORD OF IT IN MY STAR CHART!
THERE CAN BE ONLY ONE EXPLANATION-- IT IS LOCATED WHERE DARKNESS REIGNS!
DARKNESS...

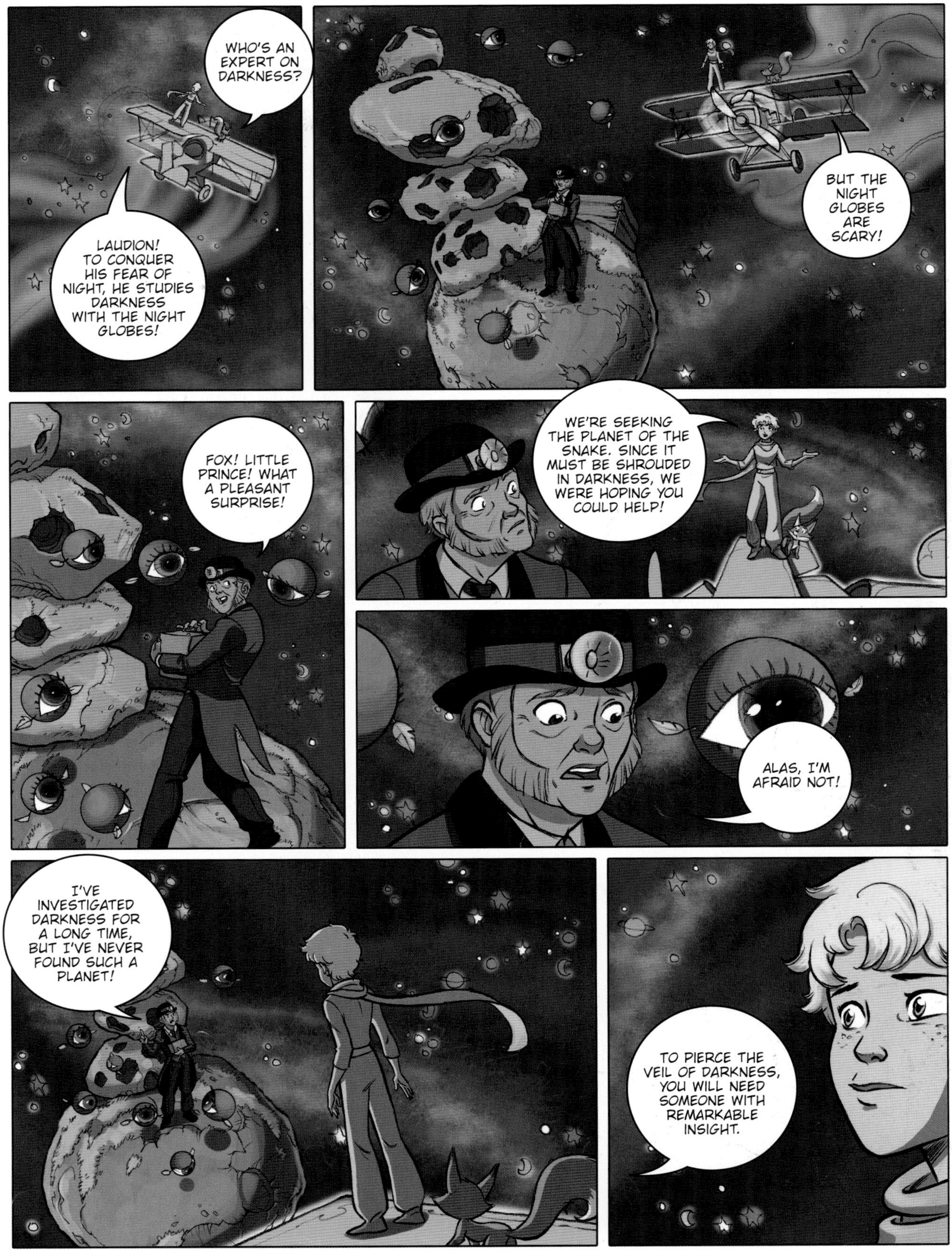
WHO'S AN EXPERT ON DARKNESS?
LAUDION! TO CONQUER HIS FEAR OF NIGHT, HE STUDIES DARKNESS WITH THE NIGHT GLOBES!
BUT THE NIGHT GLOBES ARE SCARY!
FOX! LITTLE PRINCE! WHAT A PLEASANT SURPRISE!
WE'RE SEEKING THE PLANET OF THE SNAKE. SINCE IT MUST BE SHROUDED IN DARKNESS, WE WERE HOPING YOU COULD HELP!
ALAS, I'M AFRAID NOT!
I'VE INVESTIGATED DARKNESS FOR A LONG TIME, BUT I'VE NEVER FOUND SUCH A PLANET!
TO PIERCE THE VEIL OF DARKNESS, YOU WILL NEED SOMEONE WITH REMARKABLE INSIGHT.

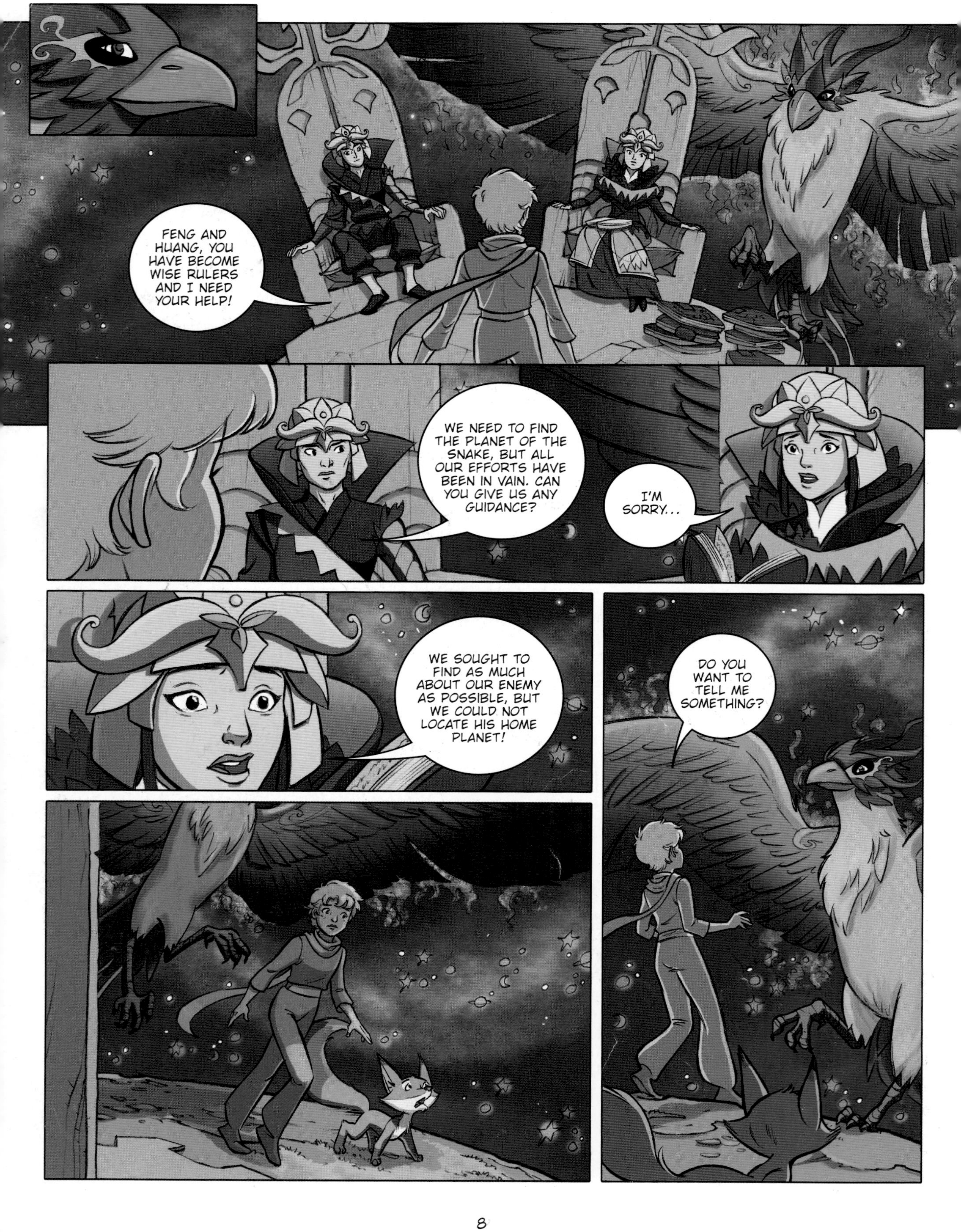
FENG AND HUANG, YOU HAVE BECOME WISE RULERS AND I NEED YOUR HELP!
WE NEED TO FIND THE PLANET OF THE SNAKE, BUT ALL OUR EFFORTS HAVE BEEN IN VAIN. CAN YOU GIVE US ANY GUIDANCE?
I'M SORRY...
WE SOUGHT TO FIND AS MUCH ABOUT OUR ENEMY AS POSSIBLE, BUT WE COULD NOT LOCATE HIS HOME PLANET!
DO YOU WANT TO TELL ME SOMETHING?

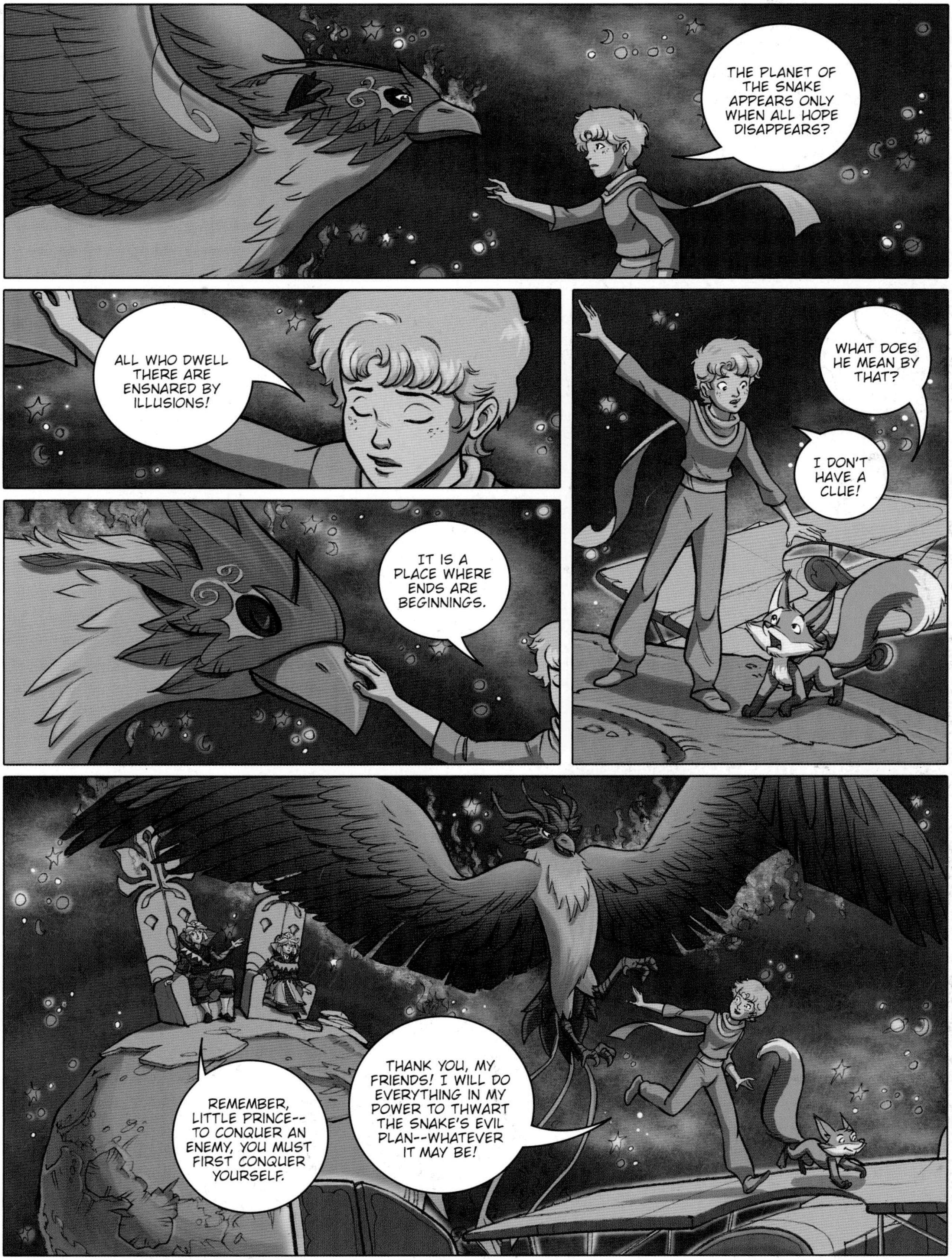
THE PLANET OF THE SNAKE APPEARS ONLY WHEN ALL HOPE DISAPPEARS?
ALL WHO DWELL THERE ARE ENSNARED BY ILLUSIONS!
IT IS A PLACE WHERE ENDS ARE BEGINNINGS.
WHAT DOES HE MEAN BY THAT?
I DON'T HAVE A CLUE!
REMEMBER, LITTLE PRINCE-- TO CONQUER AN ENEMY, YOU MUST FIRST CONQUER YOURSELF.
THANK YOU, MY FRIENDS! I WILL DO EVERYTHING IN MY POWER TO THWART THE SNAKE'S EVIL PLAN--WHATEVER IT MAY BE!

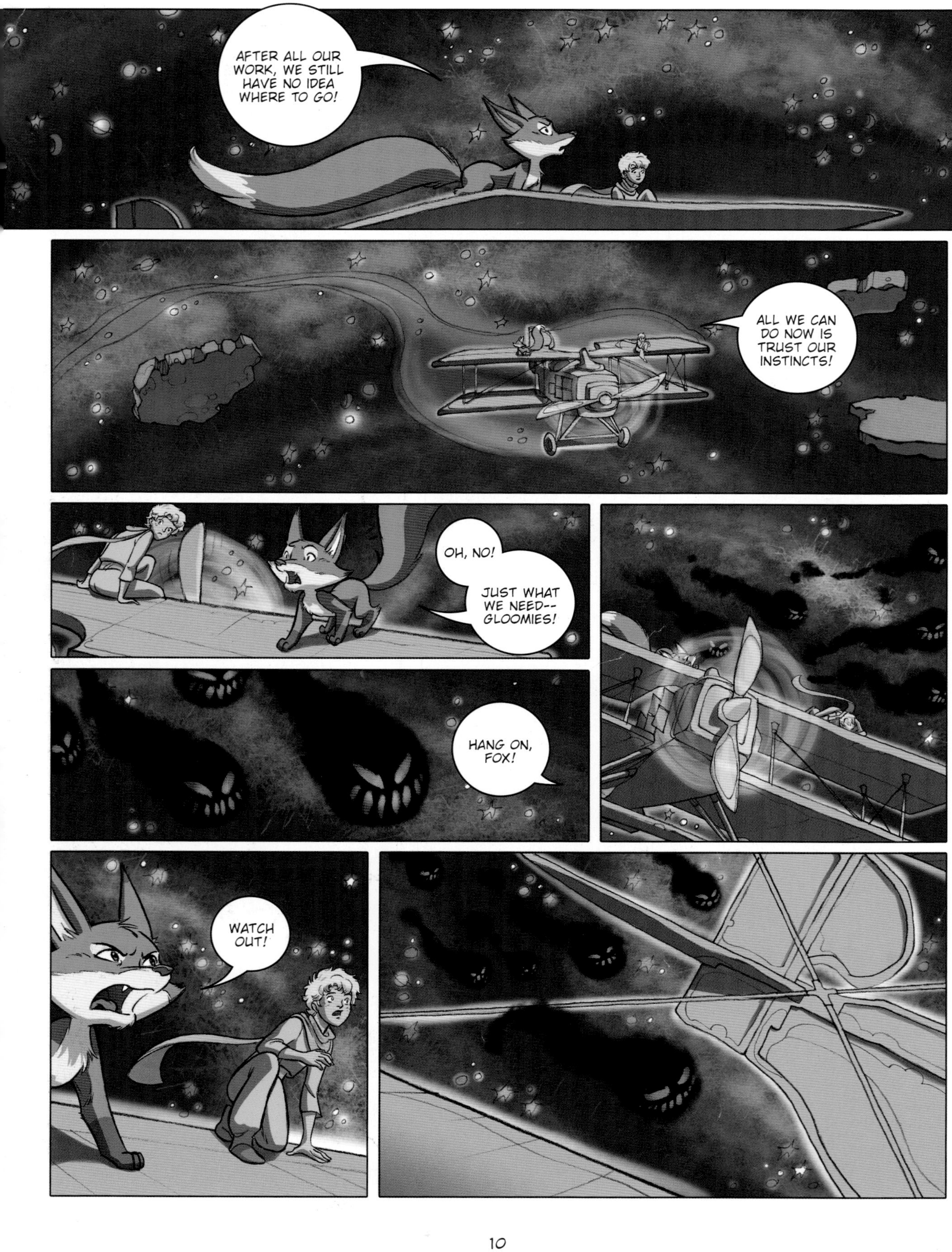
AFTER ALL OUR WORK, WE STILL HAVE NO IDEA WHERE TO GO!
ALL WE CAN DO NOW IS TRUST OUR INSTINCTS!
OH, NO!
JUST WHAT WE NEED-- GLOOMIES!
HANG ON, FOX!
WATCH OUT!

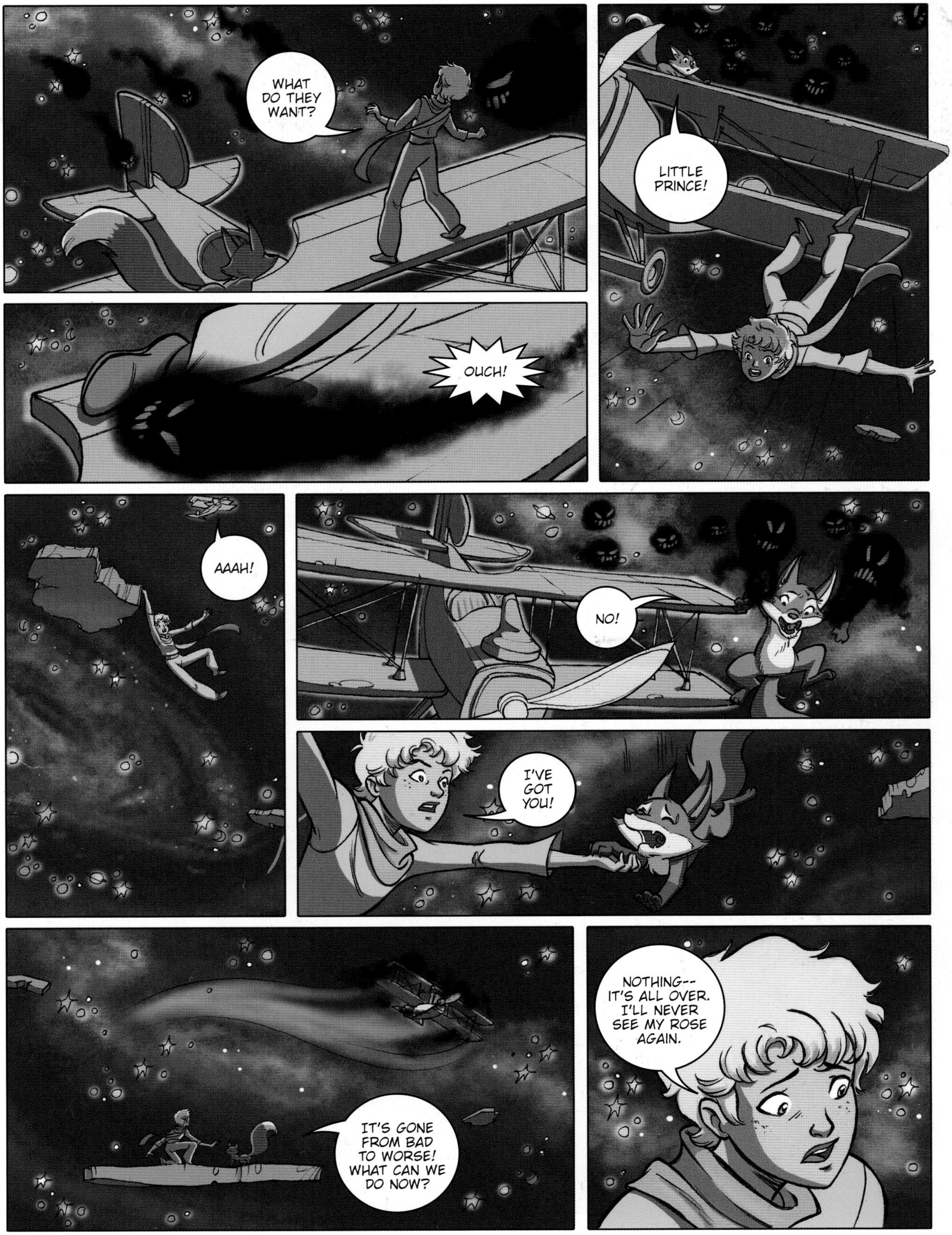
WHAT DO THEY WANT?
LITTLE PRINCE!
OUCH!
AAAH!
NO!
I'VE GOT YOU!
IT'S GONE FROM BAD TO WORSE! WHAT CAN WE DO NOW?
NOTHING-- IT'S ALL OVER. I'LL NEVER SEE MY ROSE AGAIN.

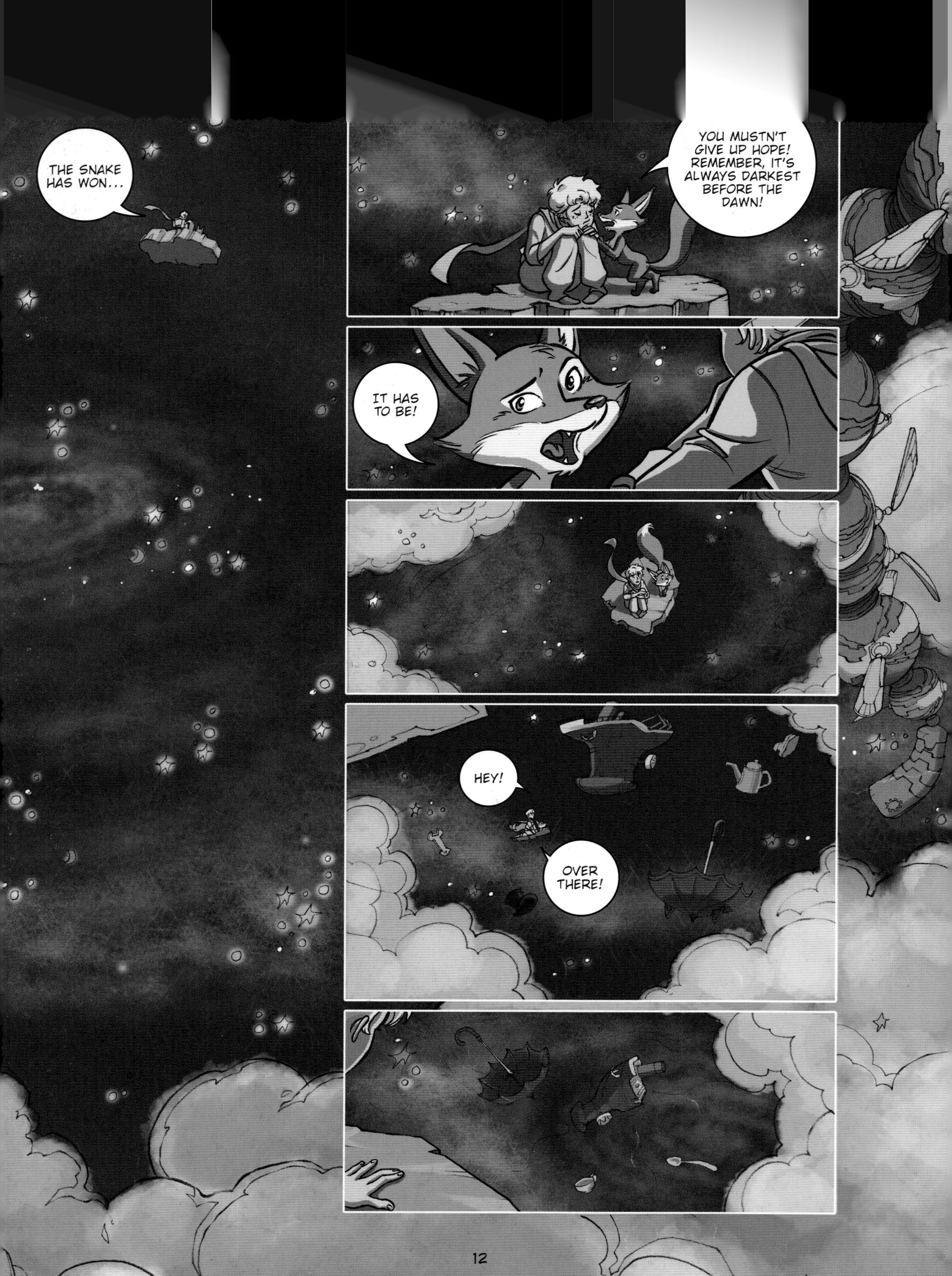
THE SNAKE HAS WON...
YOU MUSTN'T GIVE UP HOPE! REMEMBER, IT'S ALWAYS DARKEST BEFORE THE DAWN!
IT HAS TO BE!
HEY!
OVER THERE!

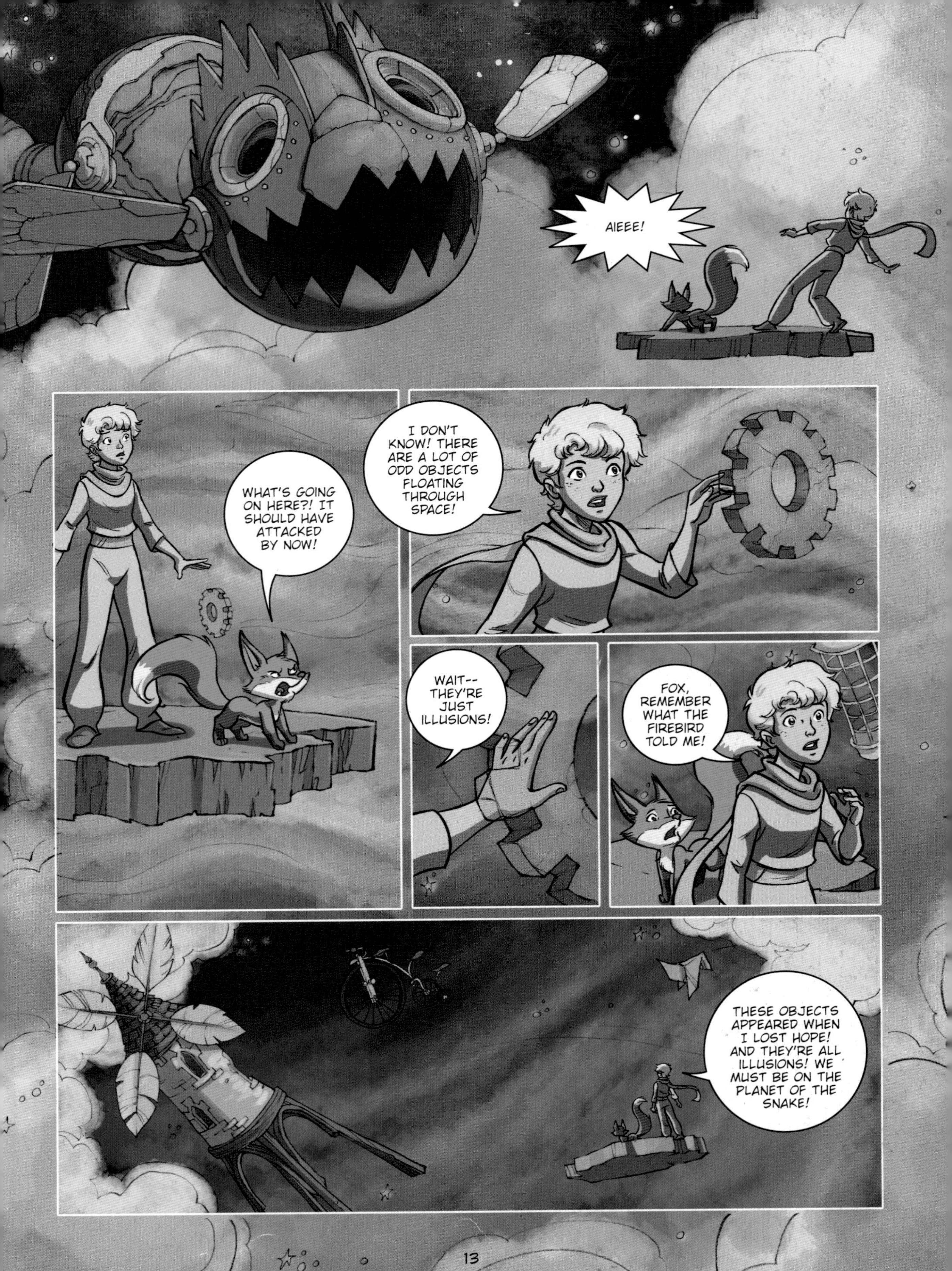
AIEEE!
WHAT'S GOING ON HERE?! IT SHOULD HAVE ATTACKED BY NOW!
I DON'T KNOW! THERE ARE A LOT OF ODD OBJECTS FLOATING THROUGH SPACE!
WAIT-- THEY'RE JUST ILLUSIONS!
FOX, REMEMBER WHAT THE FIREBIRD TOLD ME!
THESE OBJECTS APPEARED WHEN I LOST HOPE! AND THEY'RE ALL ILLUSIONS! WE MUST BE ON THE PLANET OF THE SNAKE!

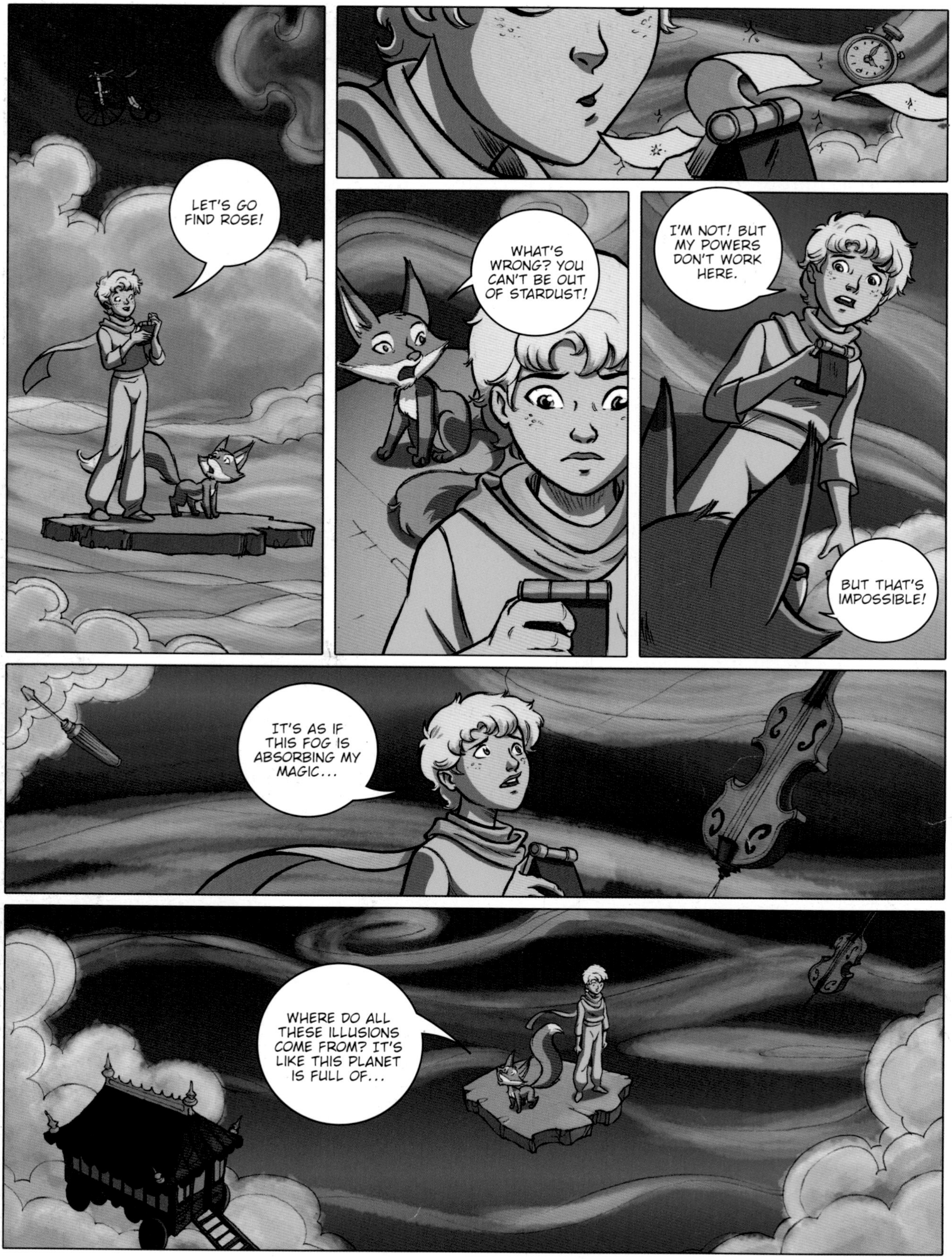
LET'S GO FIND ROSE!
WHAT'S WRONG? YOU CAN'T BE OUT OF STARDUST!
I'M NOT! BUT MY POWERS DON'T WORK HERE.
BUT THAT'S IMPOSSIBLE!
IT'S AS IF THIS FOG IS ABSORBING MY MAGIC...
WHERE DO ALL THESE ILLUSIONS COME FROM? IT'S LIKE THIS PLANET IS FULL OF...

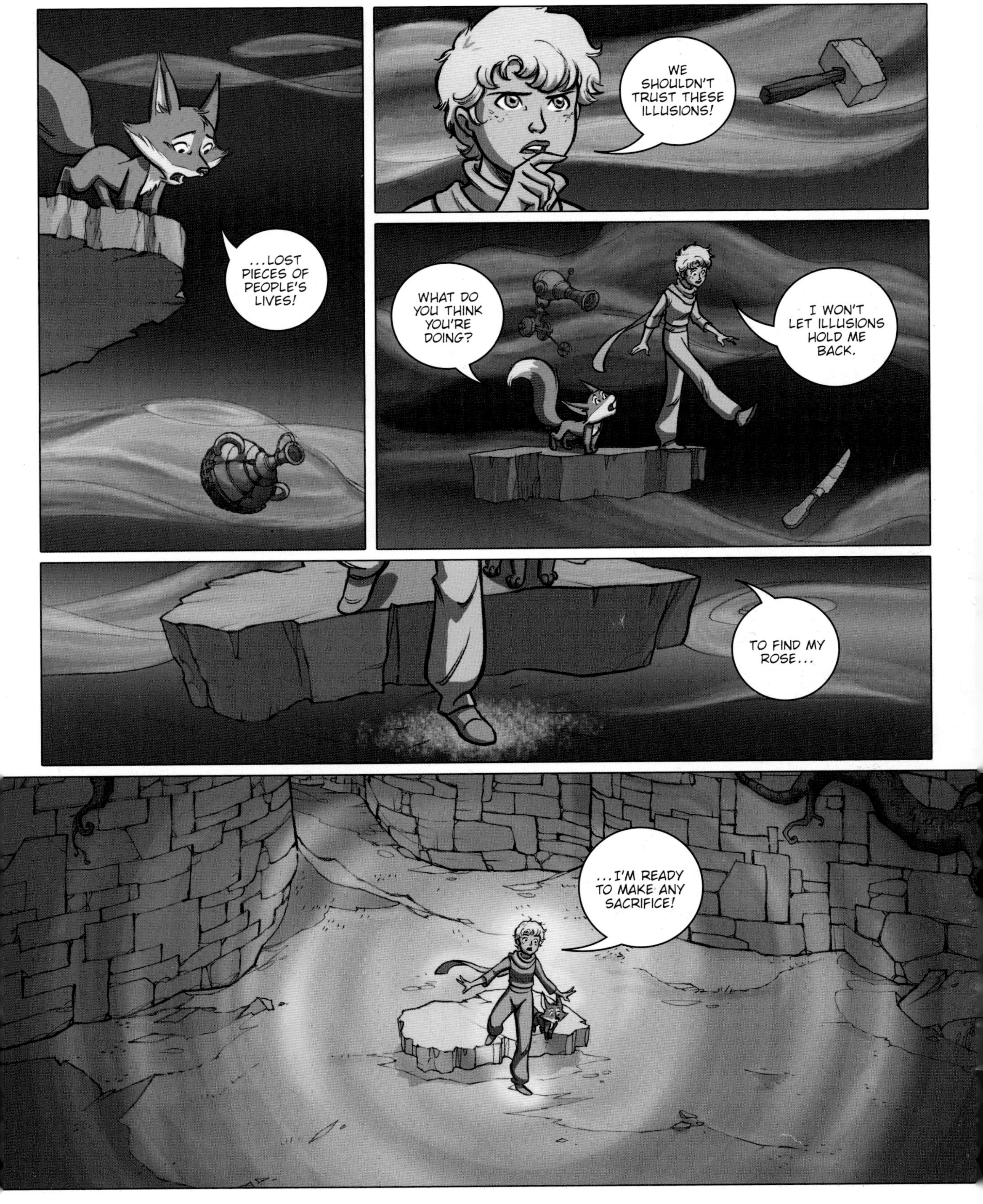
...LOST PIECES OF PEOPLE'S LIVES!
WE SHOULDN'T TRUST THESE ILLUSIONS!
WHAT DO YOU THINK YOU'RE DOING?
I WON'T LET ILLUSIONS HOLD ME BACK.
TO FIND MY ROSE...
...I'M READY TO MAKE ANY SACRIFICE!

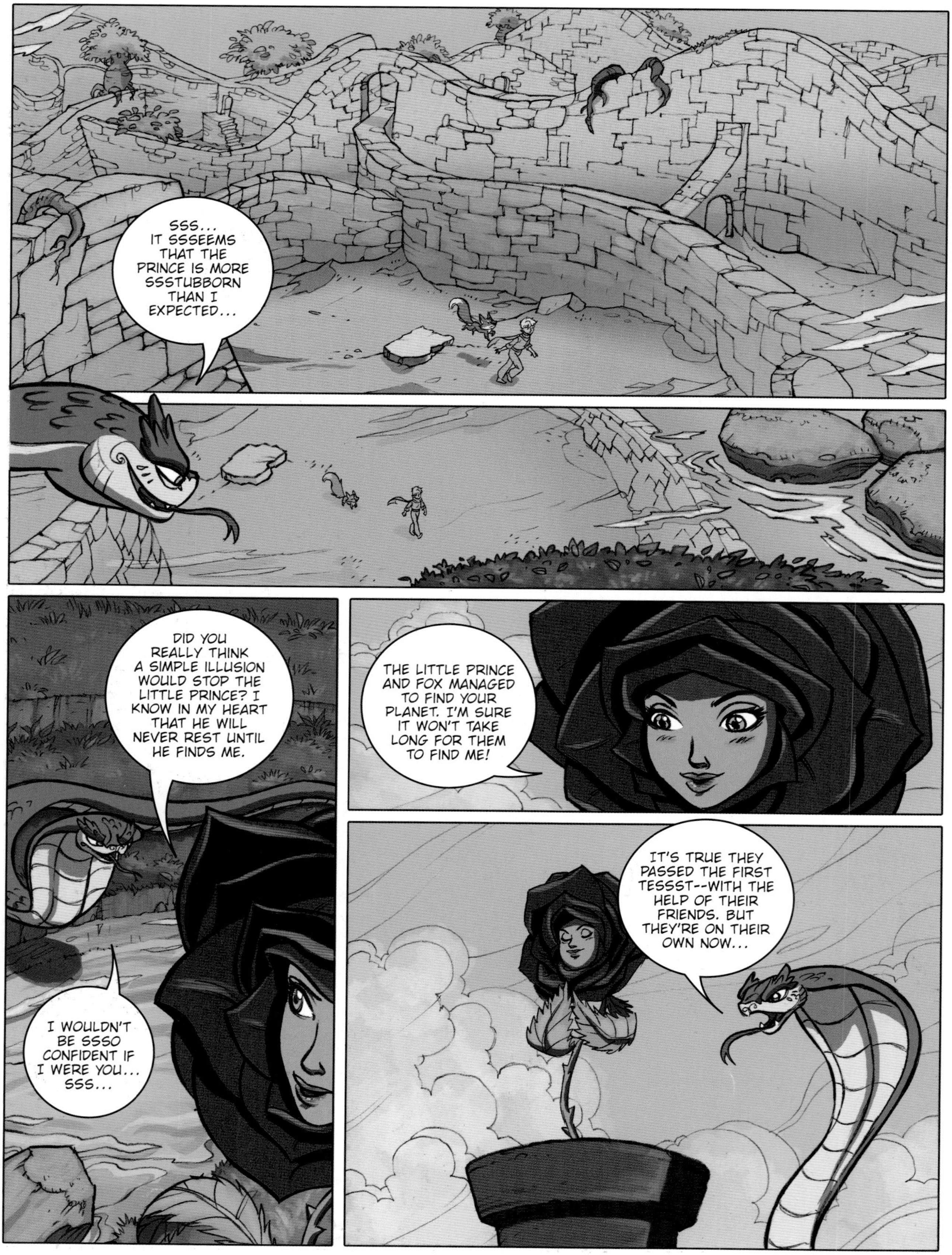
SSS... IT SSSEEMS THAT THE PRINCE IS MORE SSSTUBBORN THAN I EXPECTED...
DID YOU REALLY THINK A SIMPLE ILLUSION WOULD STOP THE LITTLE PRINCE? I KNOW IN MY HEART THAT HE WILL NEVER REST UNTIL HE FINDS ME.
I WOULDN'T BE SSSO CONFIDENT IF I WERE YOU... SSS...
THE LITTLE PRINCE AND FOX MANAGED TO FIND YOUR PLANET. I'M SURE IT WON'T TAKE LONG FOR THEM TO FIND ME!
IT'S TRUE THEY PASSED THE FIRST TESSST--WITH THE HELP OF THEIR FRIENDS. BUT THEY'RE ON THEIR OWN NOW...

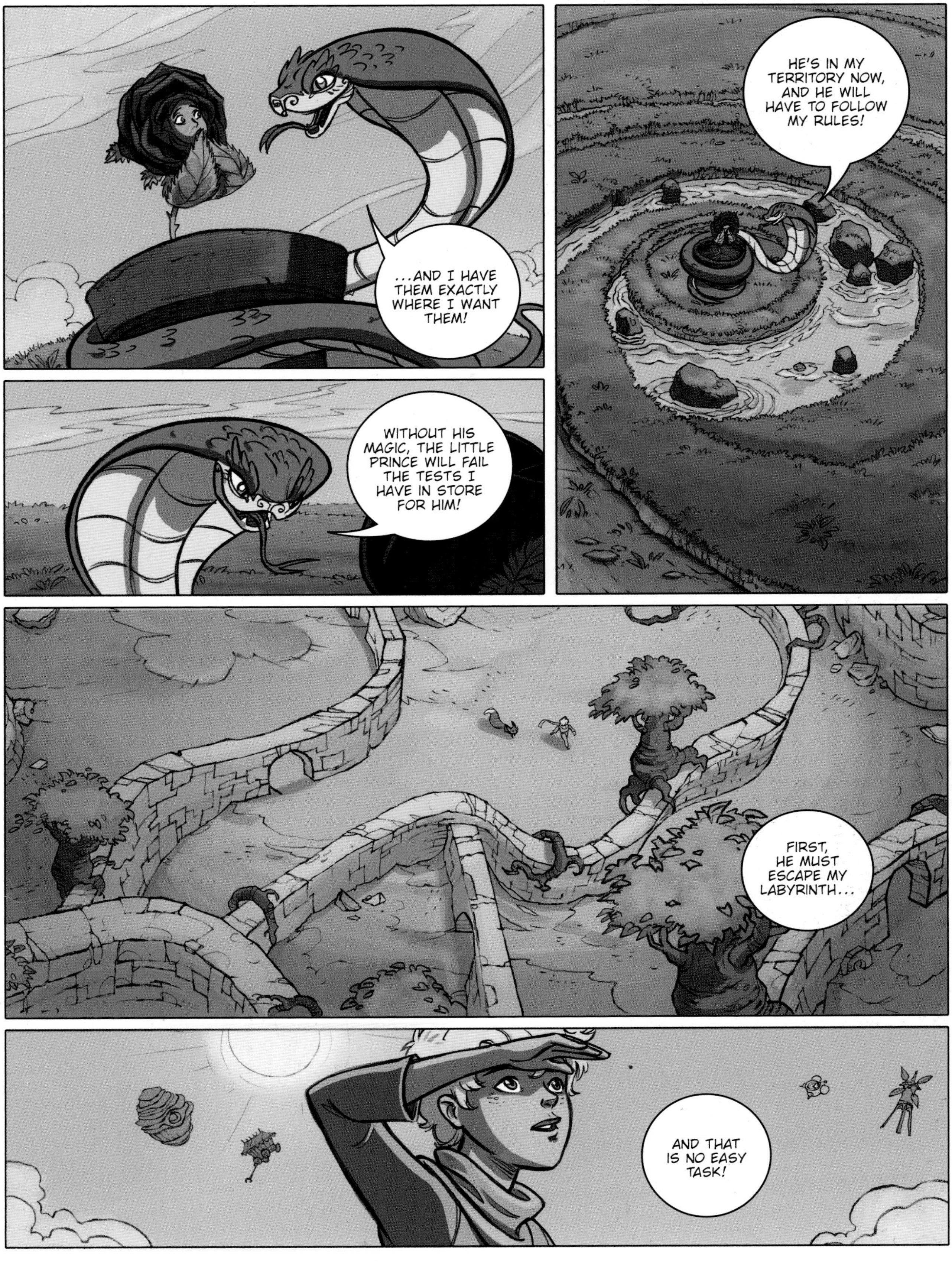
...AND I HAVE THEM EXACTLY WHERE I WANT THEM!
HE'S IN MY TERRITORY NOW, AND HE WILL HAVE TO FOLLOW MY RULES!
WITHOUT HIS MAGIC, THE LITTLE PRINCE WILL FAIL THE TESTS I HAVE IN STORE FOR HIM!
FIRST, HE MUST ESCAPE MY LABYRINTH...
AND THAT IS NO EASY TASK!

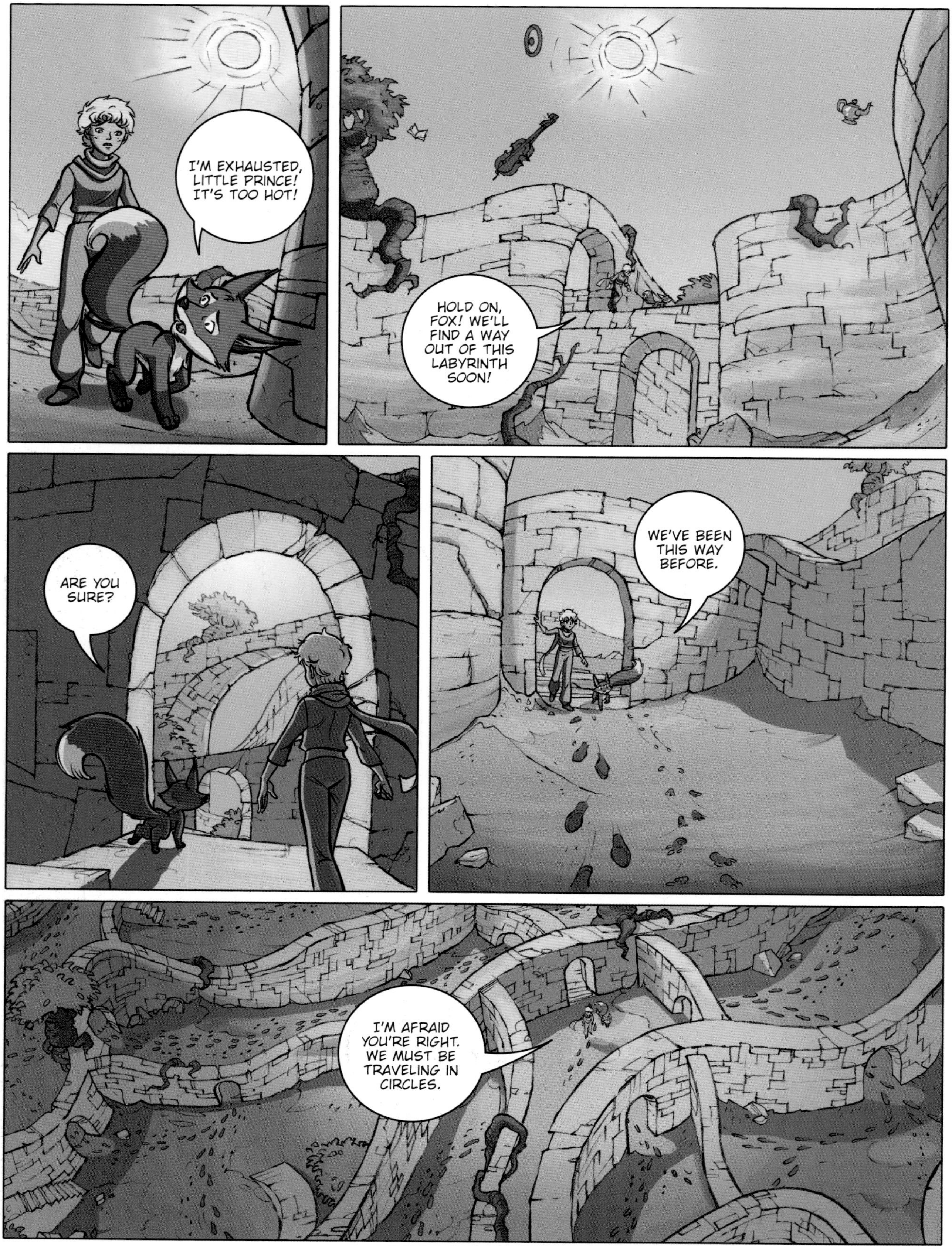
I'M EXHAUSTED, LITTLE PRINCE! IT'S TOO HOT!
HOLD ON, FOX! WE'LL FIND A WAY OUT OF THIS LABYRINTH SOON!
ARE YOU SURE?
WE'VE BEEN THIS WAY BEFORE.
I'M AFRAID YOU'RE RIGHT. WE MUST BE TRAVELING IN CIRCLES.

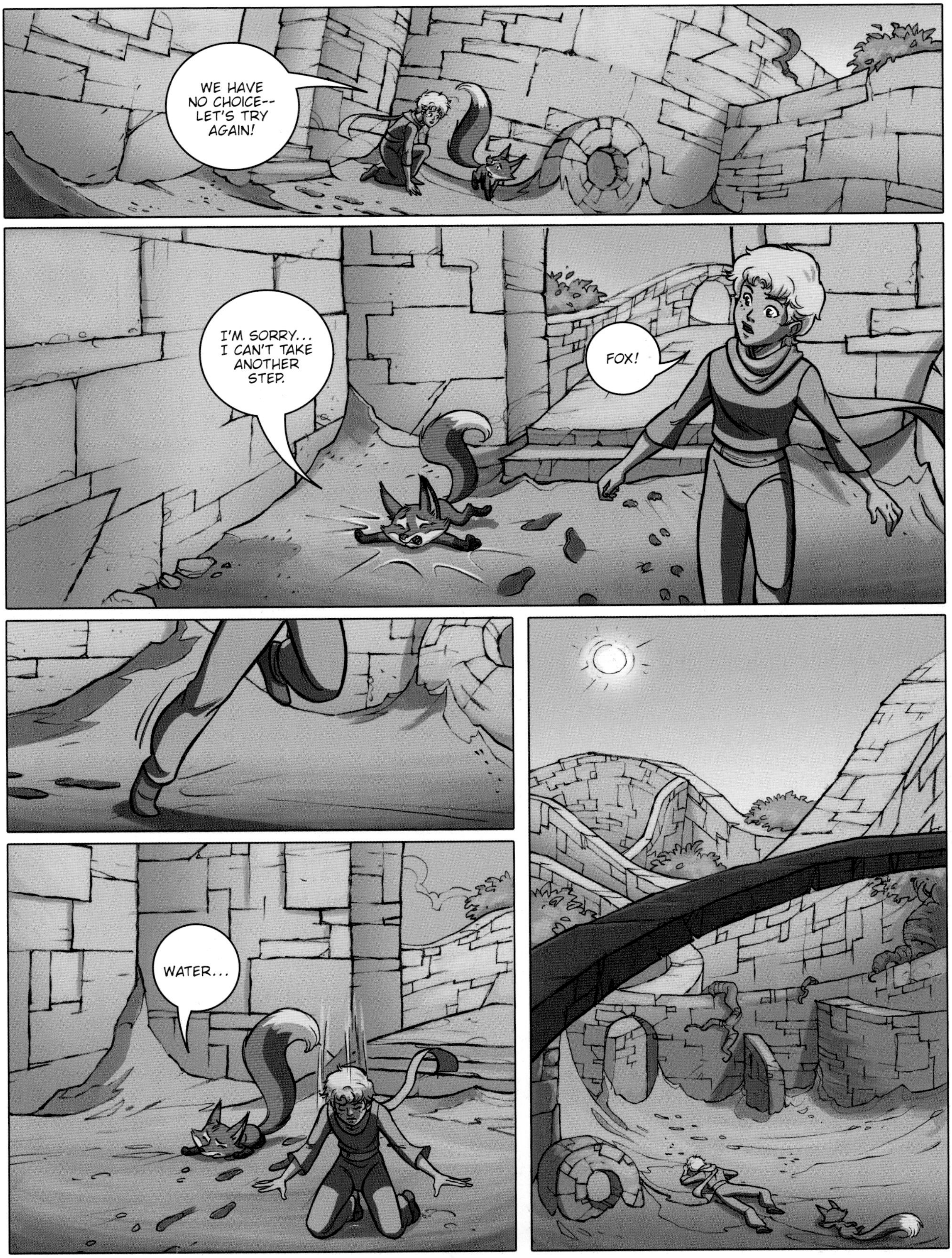
WE HAVE NO CHOICE--LET'S TRY AGAIN!
I'M SORRY... I CAN'T TAKE ANOTHER STEP.
FOX!
WATER...

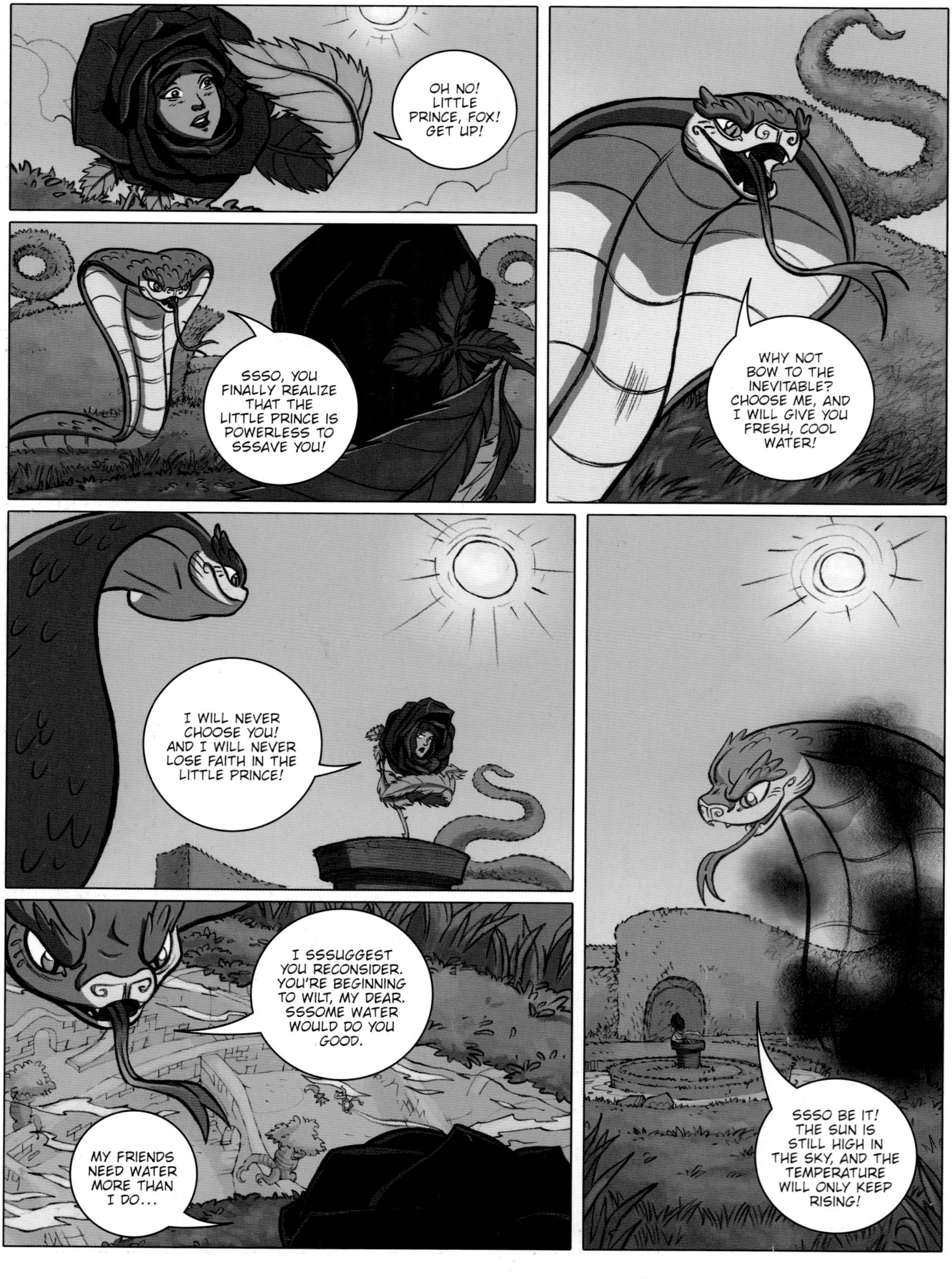
OH NO! LITTLE PRINCE, FOX! GET UP!
SSSO, YOU FINALLY REALIZE THAT THE LITTLE PRINCE IS POWERLESS TO SSSAVE YOU!
WHY NOT BOW TO THE INEVITABLE? CHOOSE ME, AND I WILL GIVE YOU FRESH, COOL WATER!
I WILL NEVER CHOOSE YOU! AND I WILL NEVER LOSE FAITH IN THE LITTLE PRINCE!
I SSSUGGEST YOU RECONSIDER. YOU'RE BEGINNING TO WILT, MY DEAR. SSSOME WATER WOULD DO YOU GOOD.
MY FRIENDS NEED WATER MORE THAN I DO...
SSSO BE IT! THE SUN IS STILL HIGH IN THE SKY, AND THE TEMPERATURE WILL ONLY KEEP RISING!

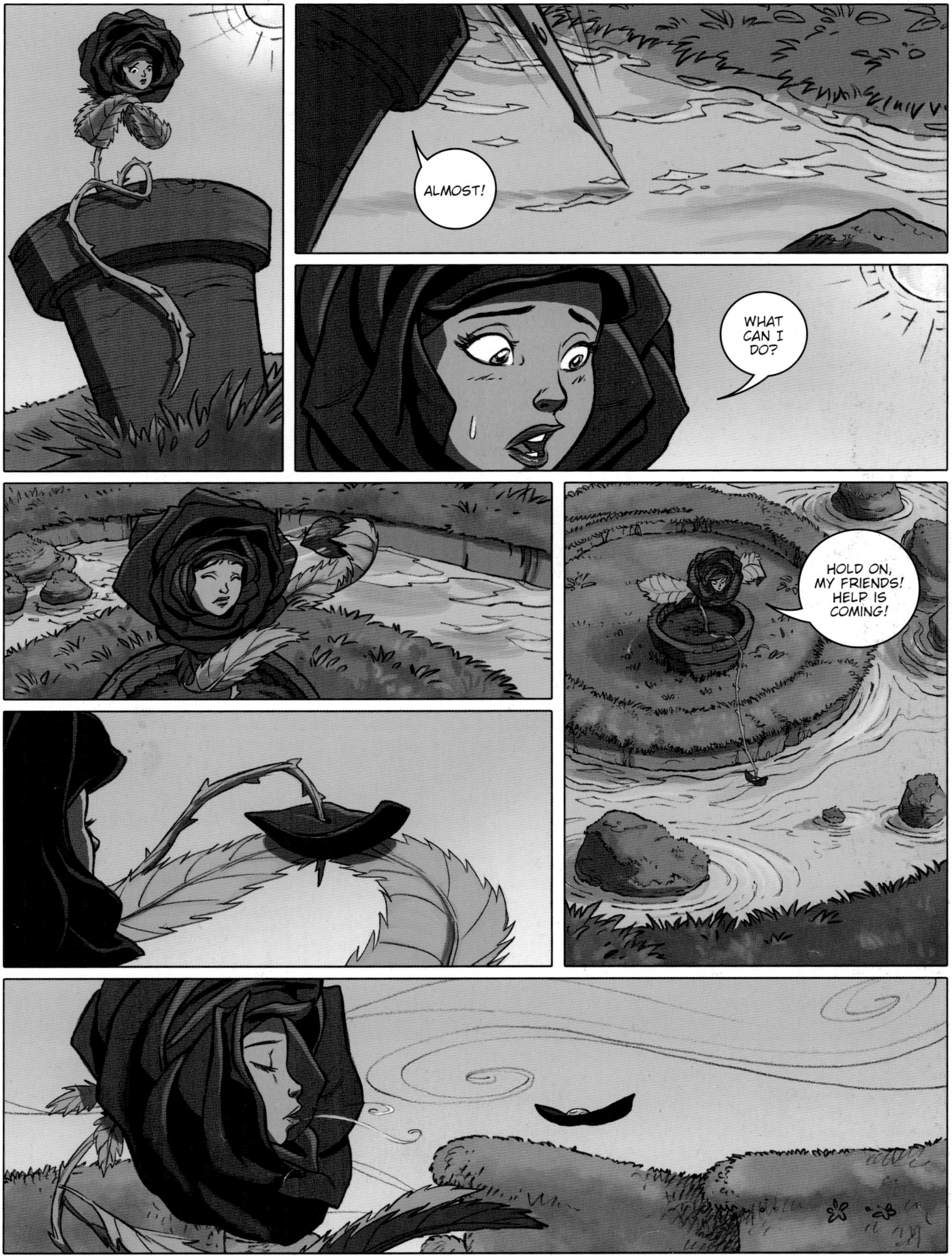
ALMOST!
WHAT CAN I DO?
HOLD ON, MY FRIENDS! HELP IS COMING!

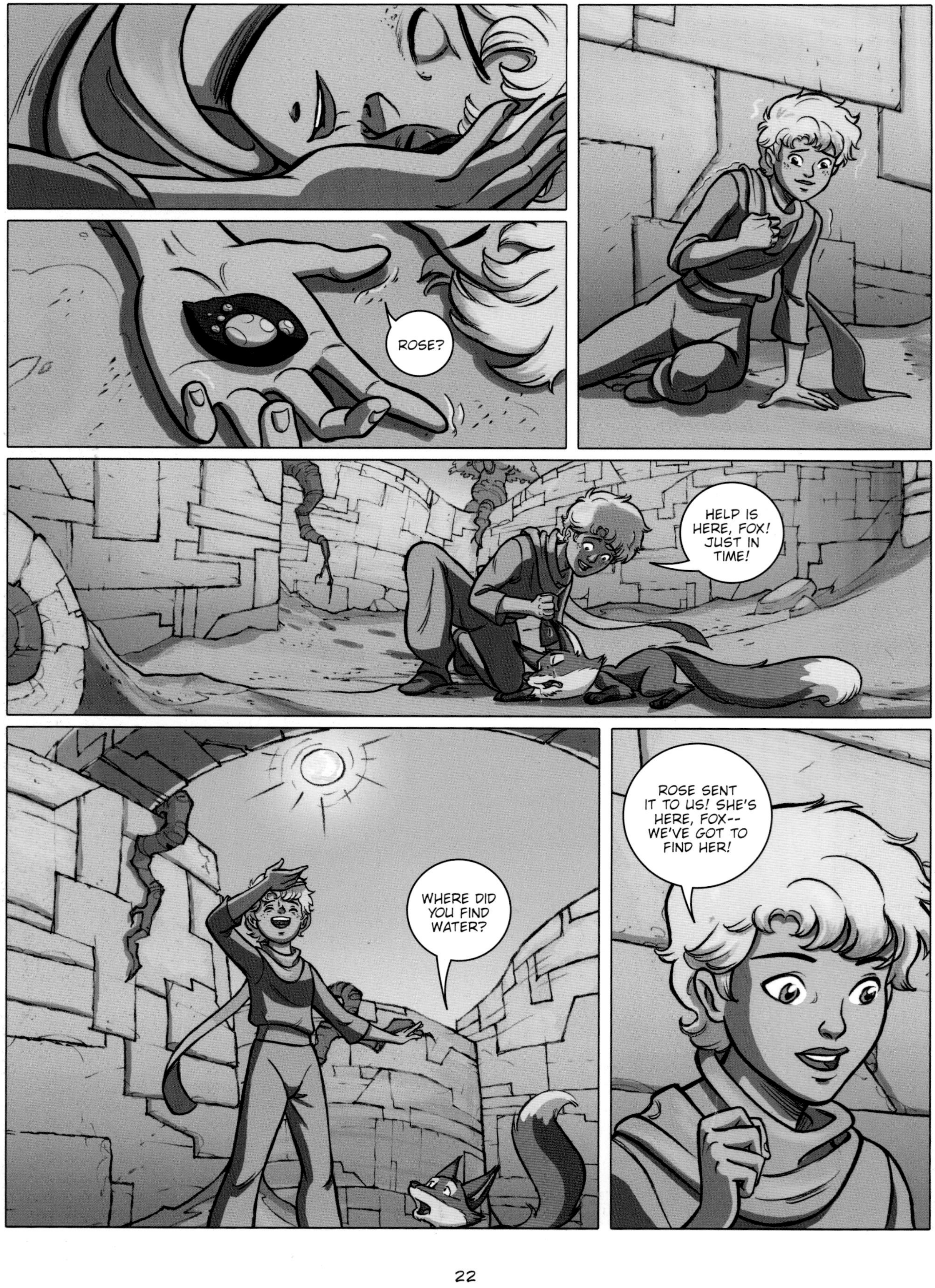
ROSE?
HELP IS HERE, FOX! JUST IN TIME!
WHERE DID YOU FIND WATER?
ROSE SENT IT TO US! SHE'S HERE, FOX-- WE'VE GOT TO FIND HER!

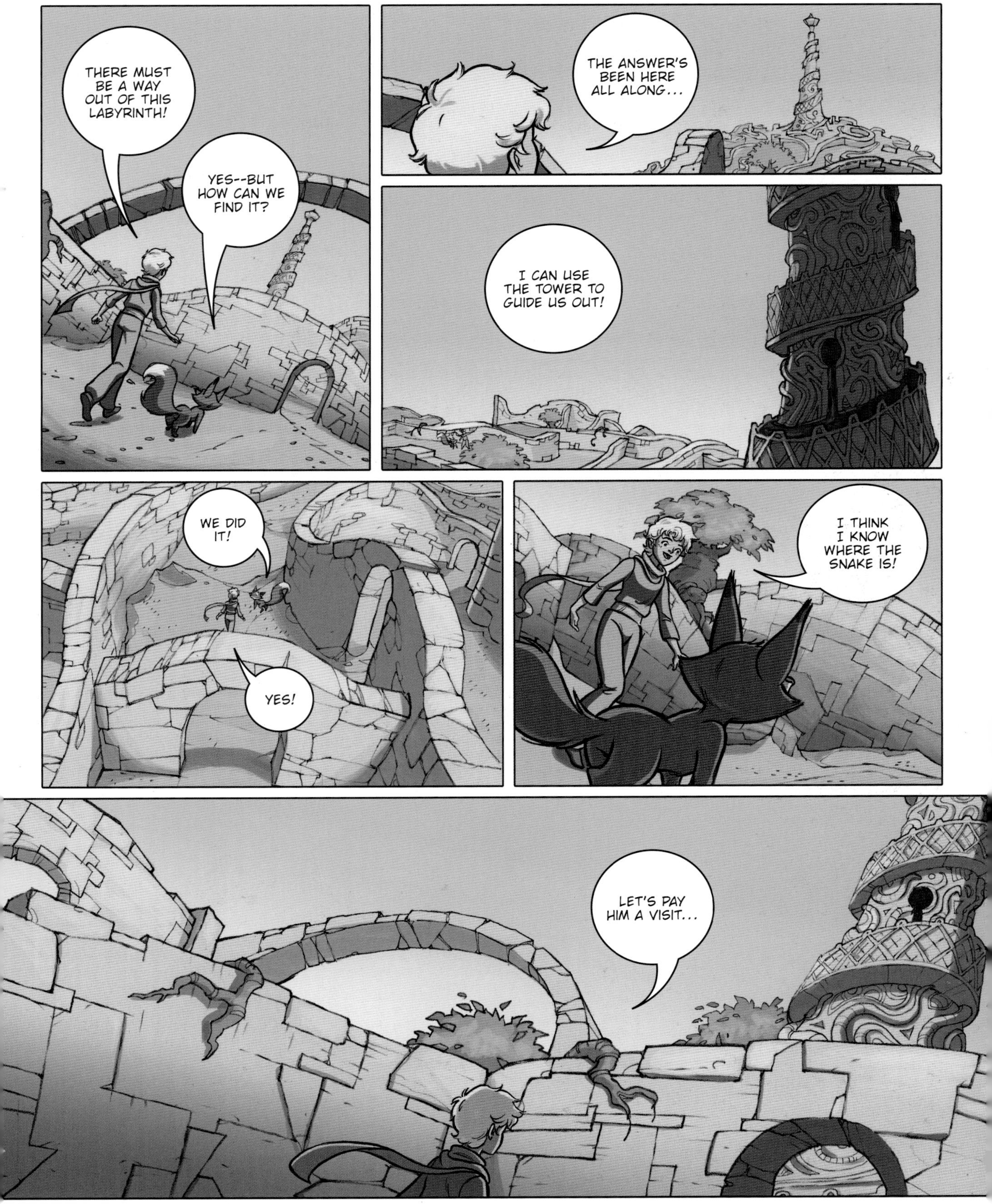
THERE MUST BE A WAY OUT OF THIS LABYRINTH!
YES--BUT HOW CAN WE FIND IT?
THE ANSWER'S BEEN HERE ALL ALONG...
I CAN USE THE TOWER TO GUIDE US OUT!
WE DID IT!
YES!
I THINK I KNOW WHERE THE SNAKE IS!
LET'S PAY HIM A VISIT...

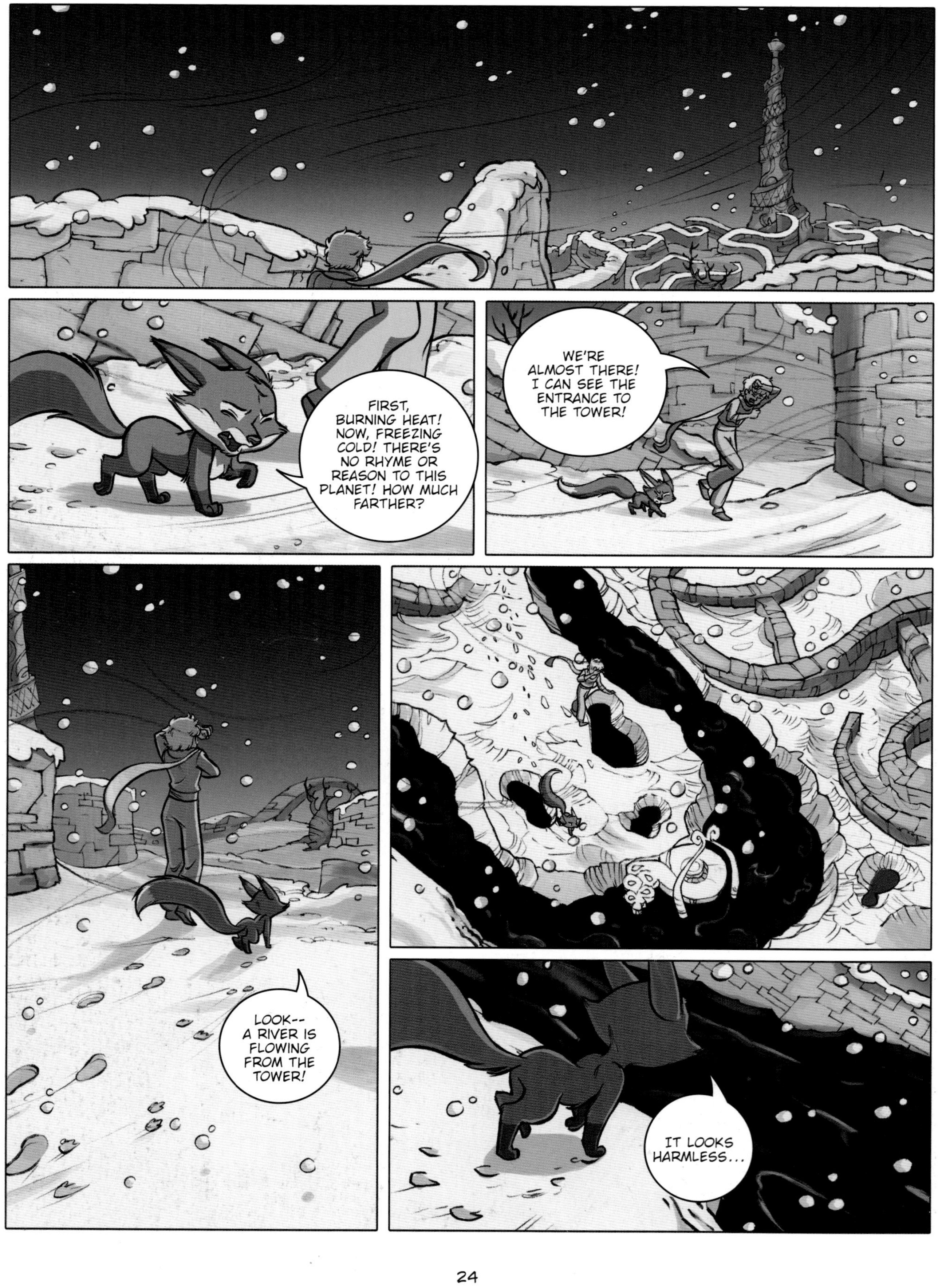
FIRST, BURNING HEAT! NOW, FREEZING COLD! THERE'S NO RHYME OR REASON TO THIS PLANET! HOW MUCH FARTHER?
WE'RE ALMOST THERE! I CAN SEE THE ENTRANCE TO THE TOWER!
LOOK-- A RIVER IS FLOWING FROM THE TOWER!
IT LOOKS HARMLESS...

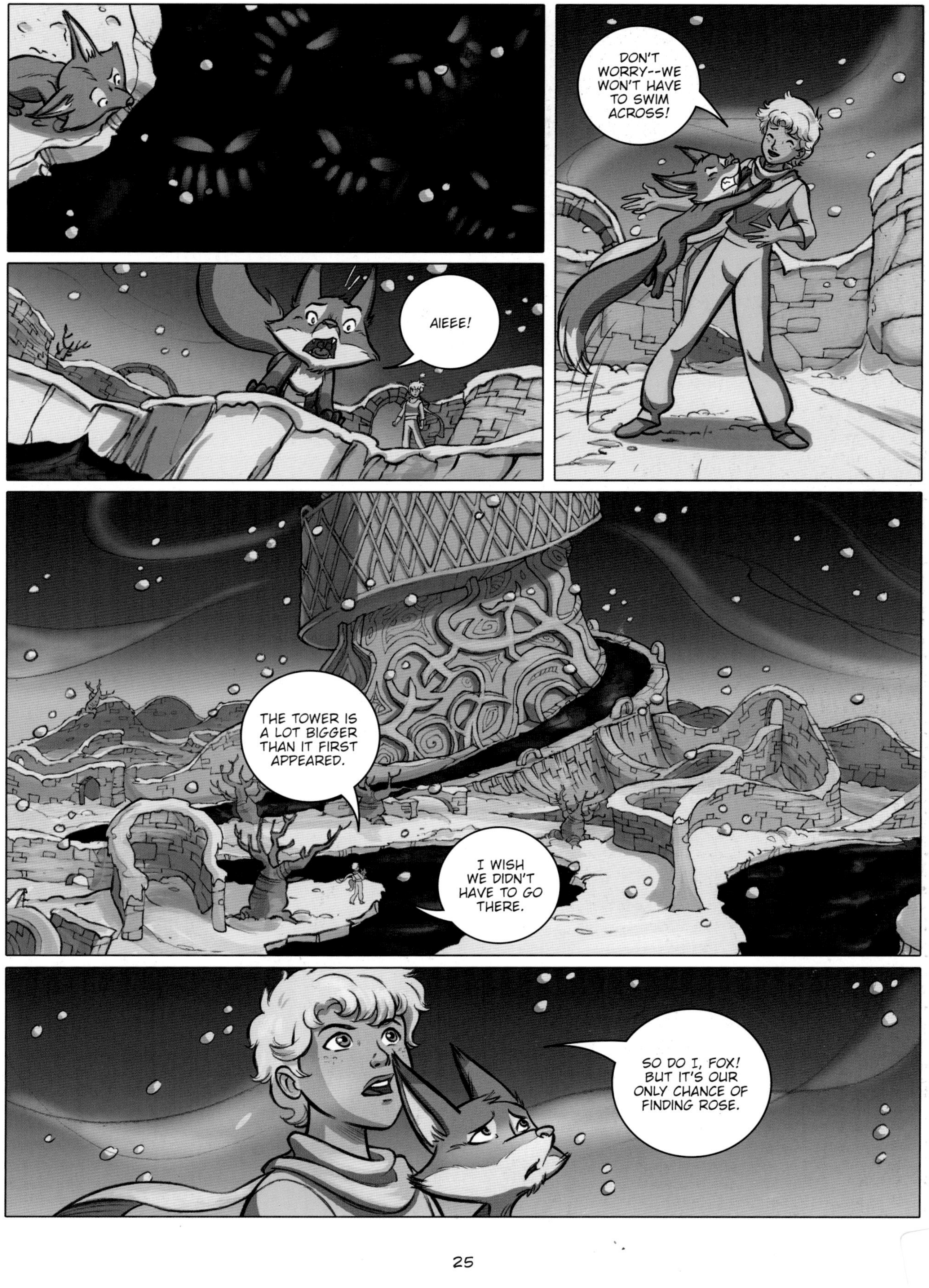
DON'T WORRY--WE WON'T HAVE TO SWIM ACROSS!
AIEEE!
THE TOWER IS A LOT BIGGER THAN IT FIRST APPEARED.
I WISH WE DIDN'T HAVE TO GO THERE.
SO DO I, FOX! BUT IT'S OUR ONLY CHANCE OF FINDING ROSE.

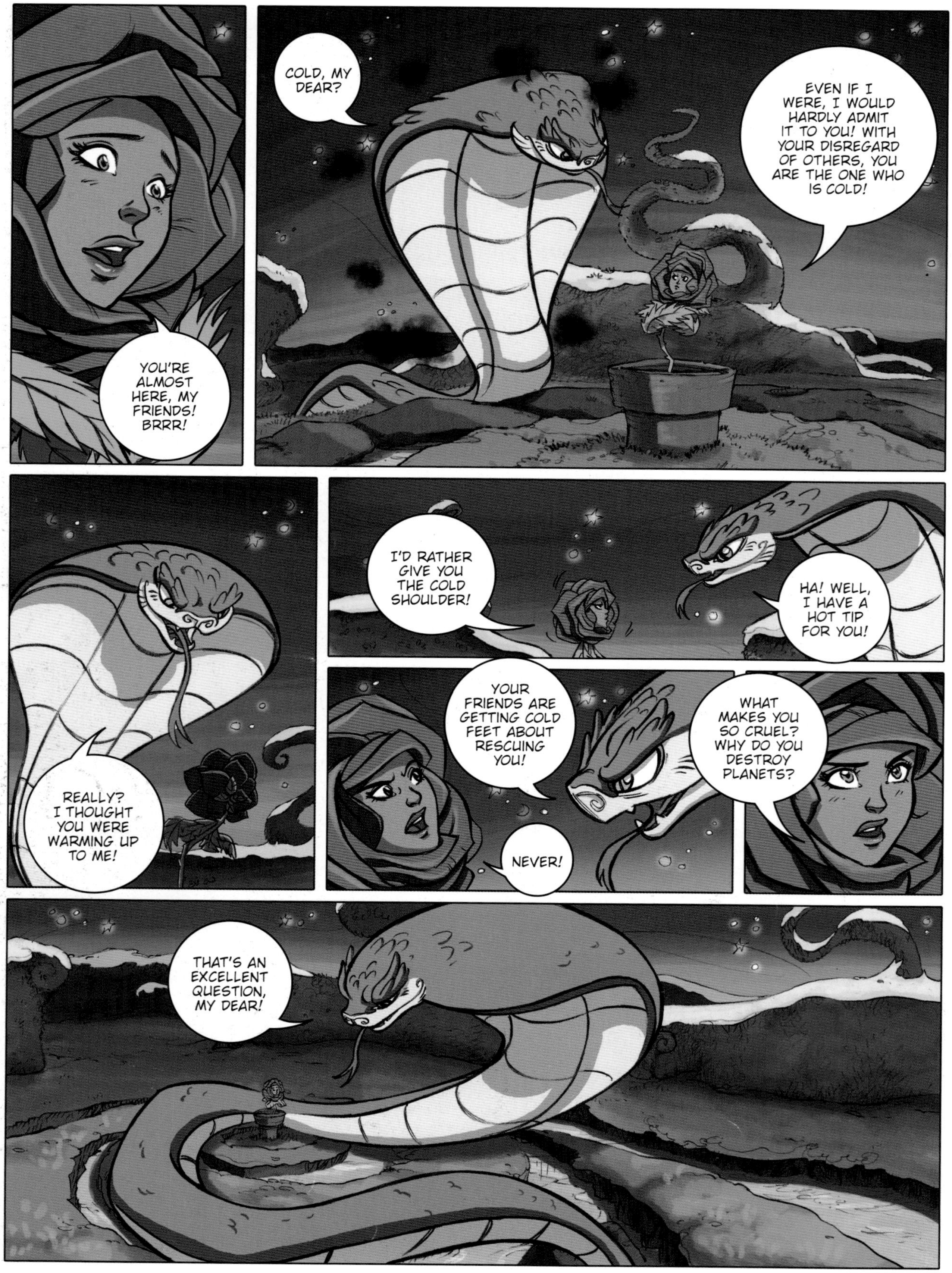
YOU'RE ALMOST HERE, MY FRIENDS! BRRR!
COLD, MY DEAR?
EVEN IF I WERE, I WOULD HARDLY ADMIT IT TO YOU! WITH YOUR DISREGARD OF OTHERS, YOU ARE THE ONE WHO IS COLD!
REALLY? I THOUGHT YOU WERE WARMING UP TO ME!
NEVER!
I'D RATHER GIVE YOU THE COLD SHOULDER!
HA! WELL, I HAVE A HOT TIP FOR YOU!
YOUR FRIENDS ARE GETTING COLD FEET ABOUT RESCUING YOU!
WHAT MAKES YOU SO CRUEL? WHY DO YOU DESTROY PLANETS?
THAT'S AN EXCELLENT QUESTION, MY DEAR!

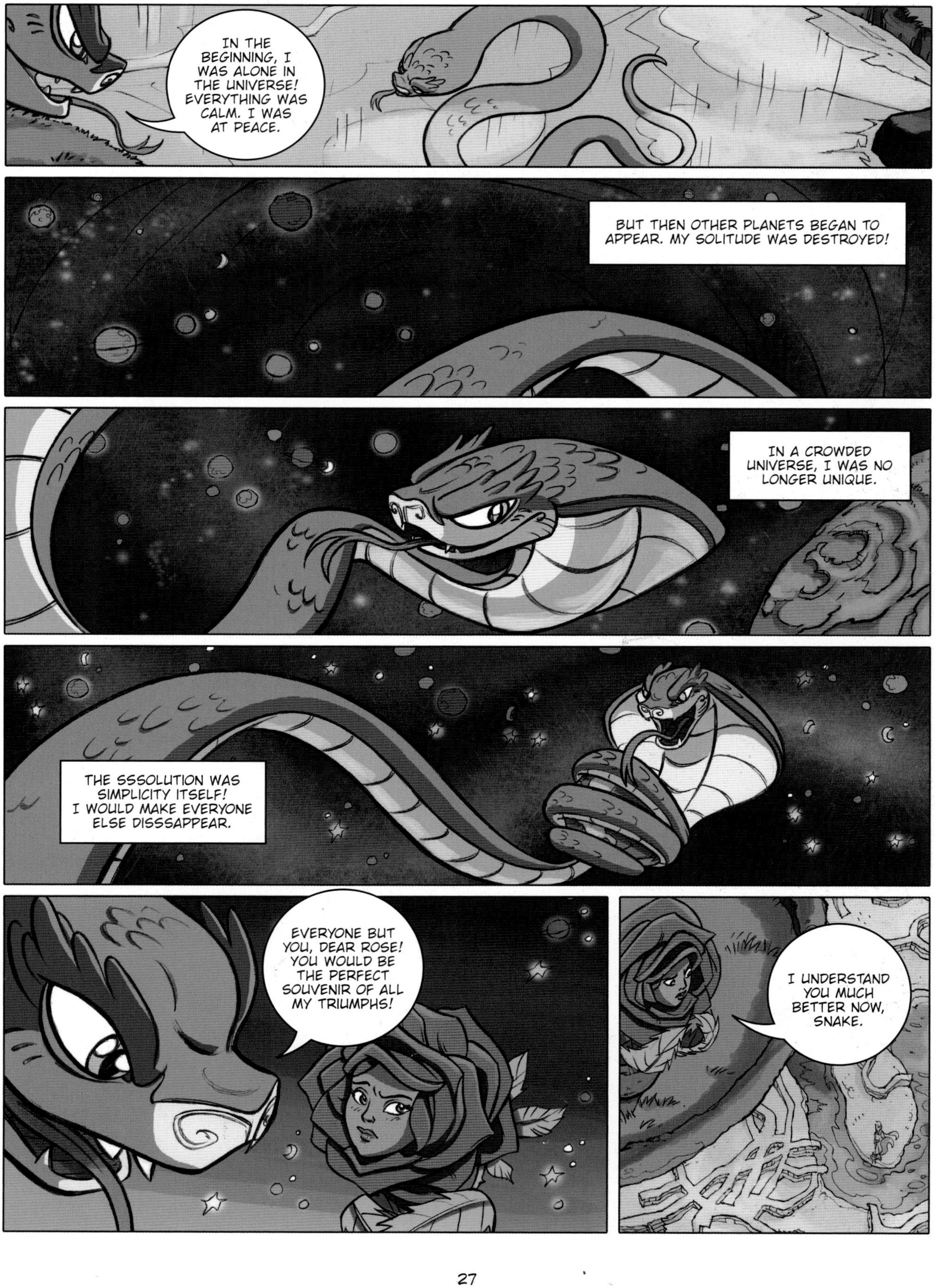
IN THE BEGINNING, I WAS ALONE IN THE UNIVERSE! EVERYTHING WAS CALM. I WAS AT PEACE.
BUT THEN OTHER PLANETS BEGAN TO APPEAR. MY SOLITUDE WAS DESTROYED!
IN A CROWDED UNIVERSE, I WAS NO LONGER UNIQUE.
THE SSSOLUTION WAS SIMPLICITY ITSELF! I WOULD MAKE EVERYONE ELSE DISSSAPPEAR.
EVERYONE BUT YOU, DEAR ROSE! YOU WOULD BE THE PERFECT SOUVENIR OF ALL MY TRIUMPHS!
I UNDERSTAND YOU MUCH BETTER NOW, SNAKE.

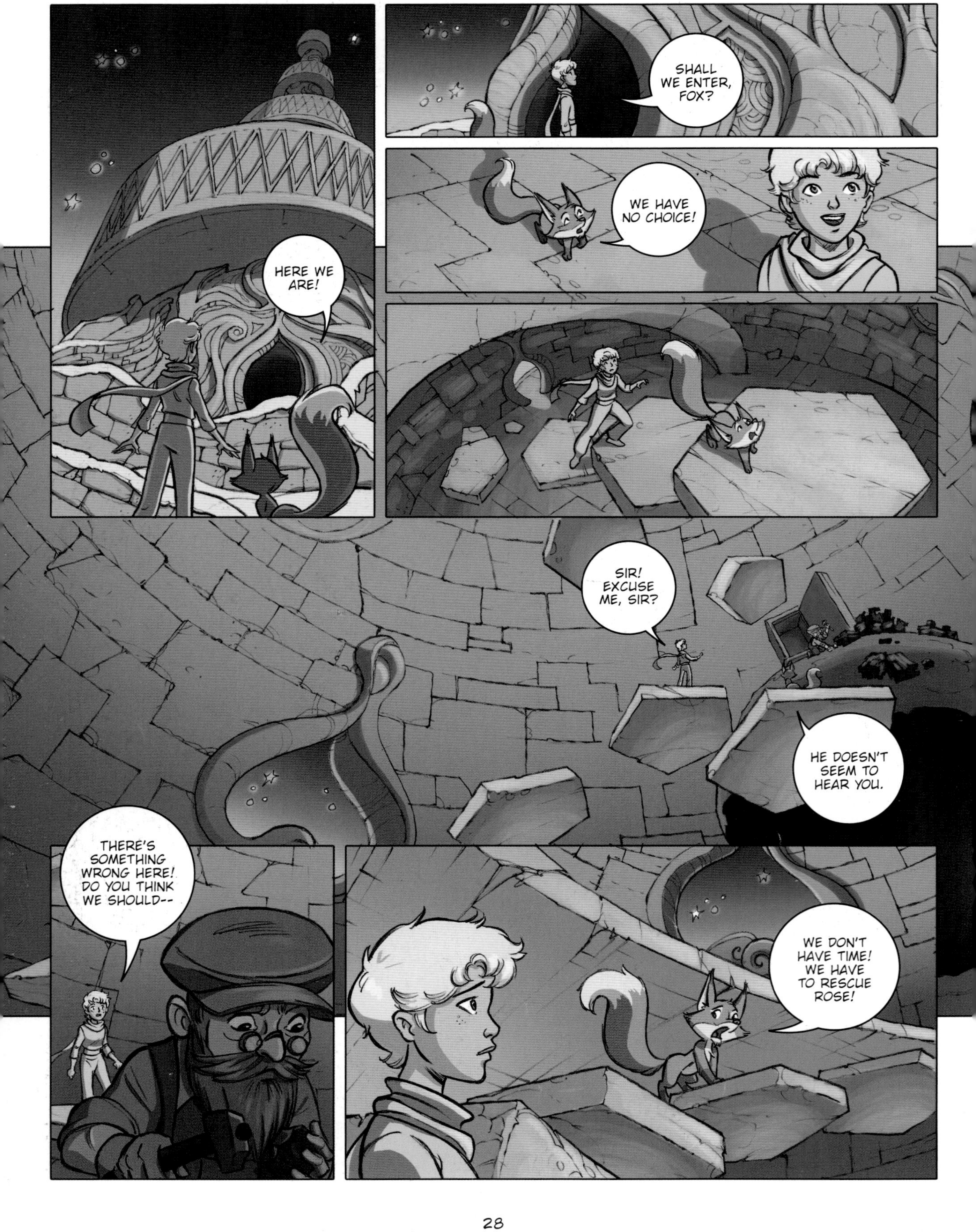
HERE WE ARE!
SHALL WE ENTER, FOX?
WE HAVE NO CHOICE!
SIR! EXCUSE ME, SIR?
HE DOESN'T SEEM TO HEAR YOU.
THERE'S SOMETHING WRONG HERE! DO YOU THINK WE SHOULD--
WE DON'T HAVE TIME! WE HAVE TO RESCUE ROSE!

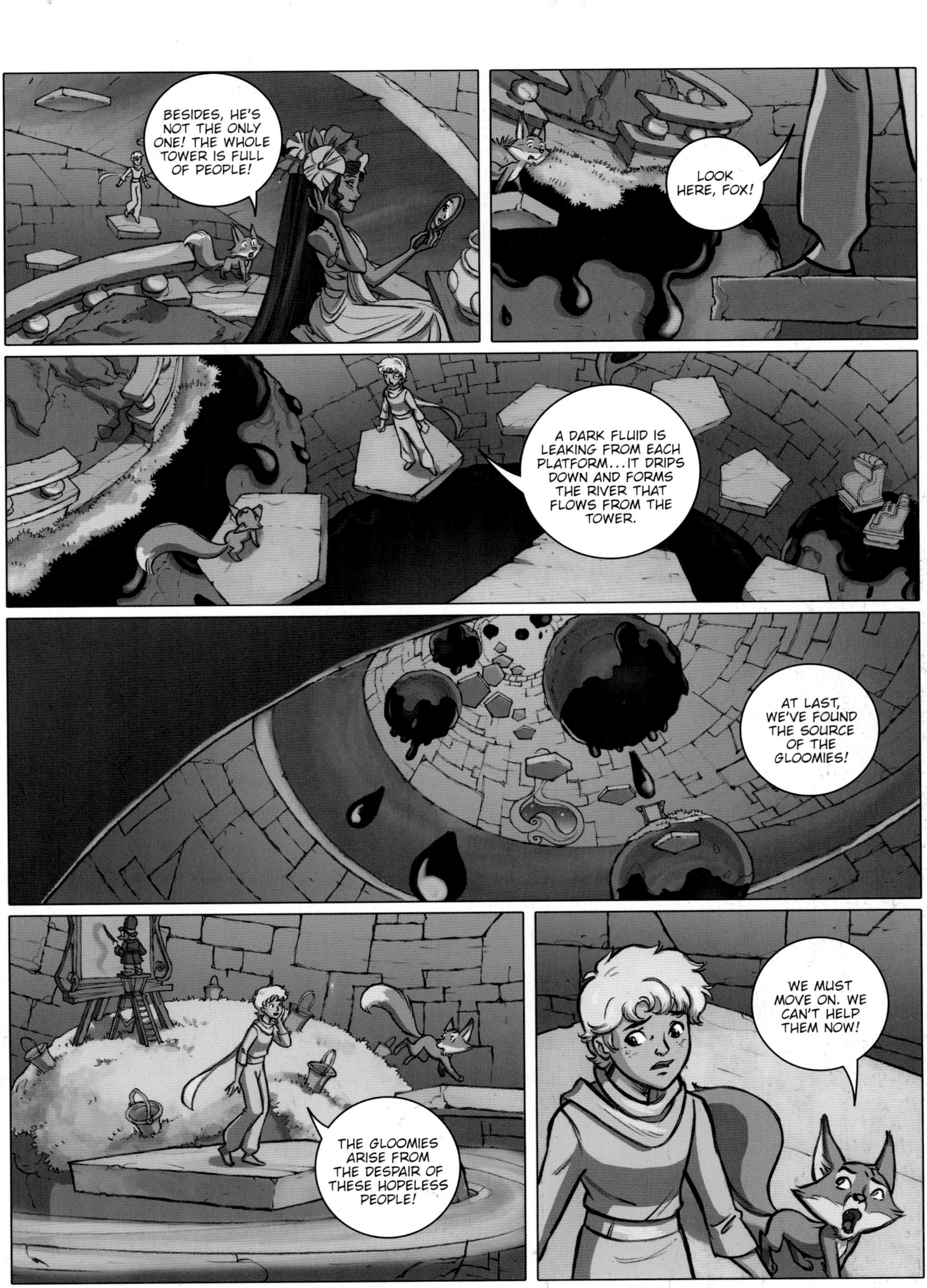
BESIDES, HE'S NOT THE ONLY ONE! THE WHOLE TOWER IS FULL OF PEOPLE!
LOOK HERE, FOX!
A DARK FLUID IS LEAKING FROM EACH PLATFORM...IT DRIPS DOWN AND FORMS THE RIVER THAT FLOWS FROM THE TOWER.
AT LAST, WE'VE FOUND THE SOURCE OF THE GLOOMIES!
THE GLOOMIES ARISE FROM THE DESPAIR OF THESE HOPELESS PEOPLE!
WE MUST MOVE ON. WE CAN'T HELP THEM NOW!

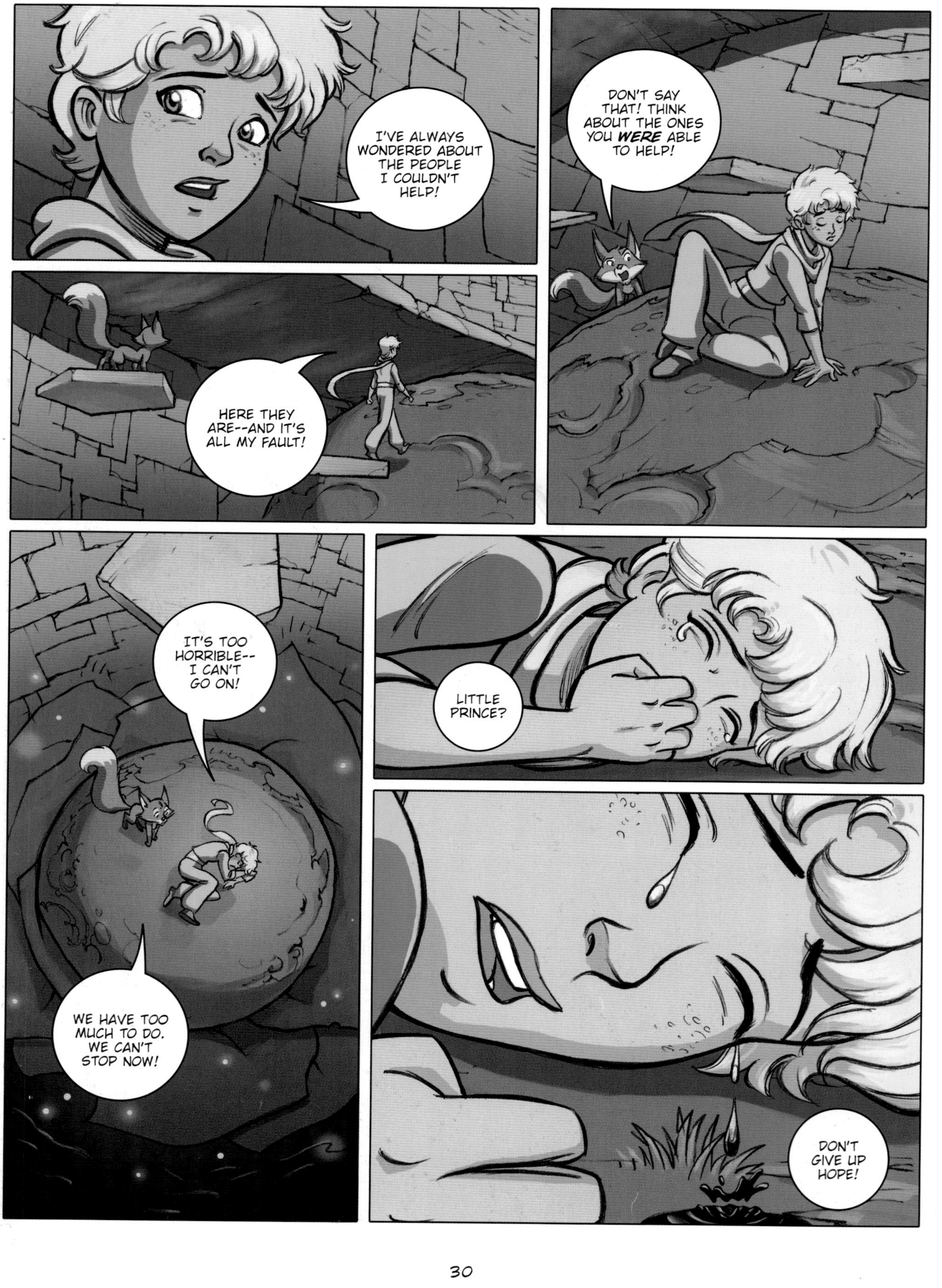
I'VE ALWAYS WONDERED ABOUT THE PEOPLE I COULDN'T HELP!
DON'T SAY THAT! THINK ABOUT THE ONES YOU ***WERE*** ABLE TO HELP!
HERE THEY ARE--AND IT'S ALL MY FAULT!
IT'S TOO HORRIBLE--I CAN'T GO ON!
WE HAVE TOO MUCH TO DO. WE CAN'T STOP NOW!
LITTLE PRINCE?
DON'T GIVE UP HOPE!

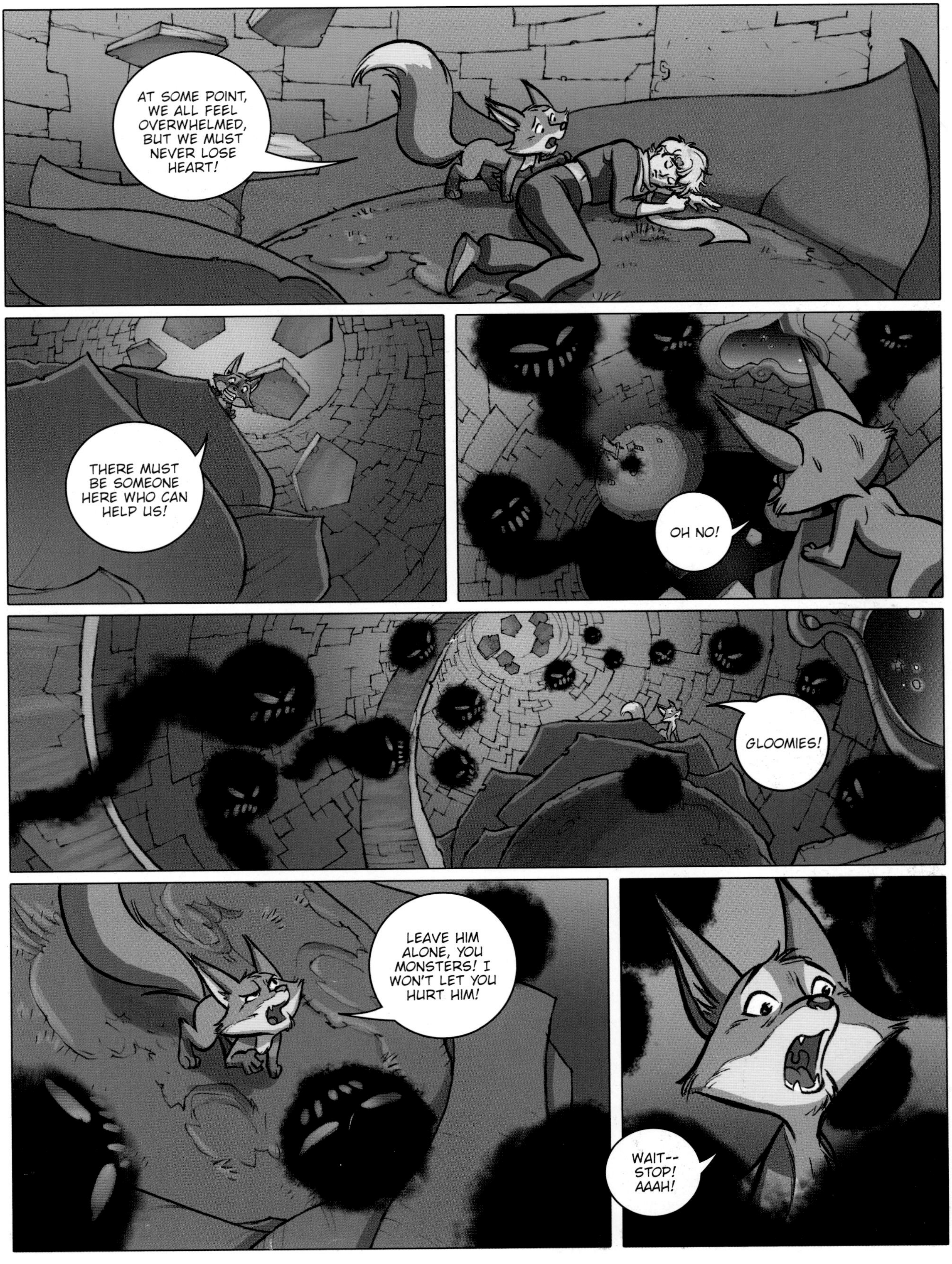
AT SOME POINT, WE ALL FEEL OVERWHELMED, BUT WE MUST NEVER LOSE HEART!
THERE MUST BE SOMEONE HERE WHO CAN HELP US!
OH NO!
GLOOMIES!
LEAVE HIM ALONE, YOU MONSTERS! I WON'T LET YOU HURT HIM!
WAIT-- STOP! AAAH!

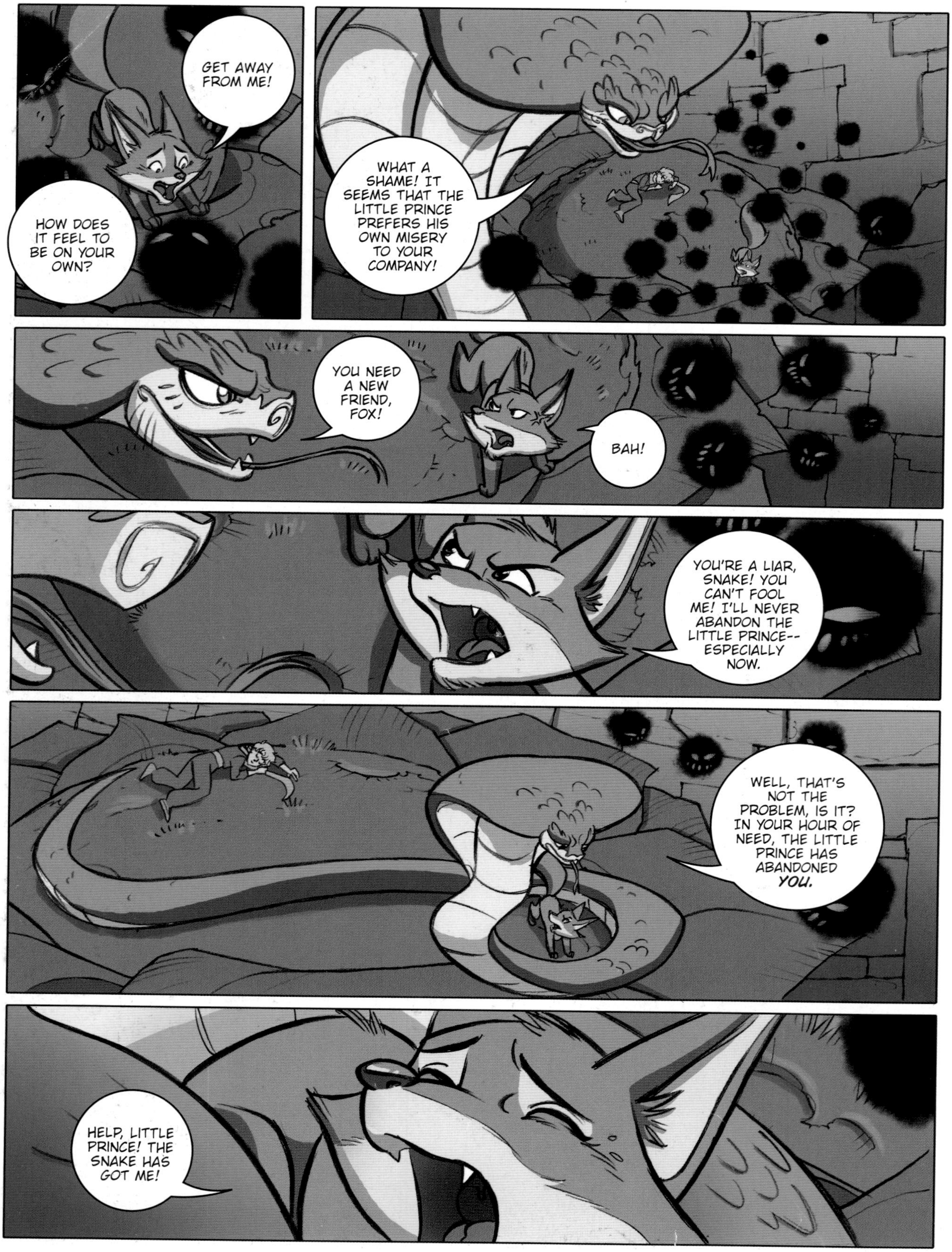
GET AWAY FROM ME!
HOW DOES IT FEEL TO BE ON YOUR OWN?
WHAT A SHAME! IT SEEMS THAT THE LITTLE PRINCE PREFERS HIS OWN MISERY TO YOUR COMPANY!
YOU NEED A NEW FRIEND, FOX!
BAH!
YOU'RE A LIAR, SNAKE! YOU CAN'T FOOL ME! I'LL NEVER ABANDON THE LITTLE PRINCE-- ESPECIALLY NOW.
WELL, THAT'S NOT THE PROBLEM, IS IT? IN YOUR HOUR OF NEED, THE LITTLE PRINCE HAS ABANDONED YOU.
HELP, LITTLE PRINCE! THE SNAKE HAS GOT ME!

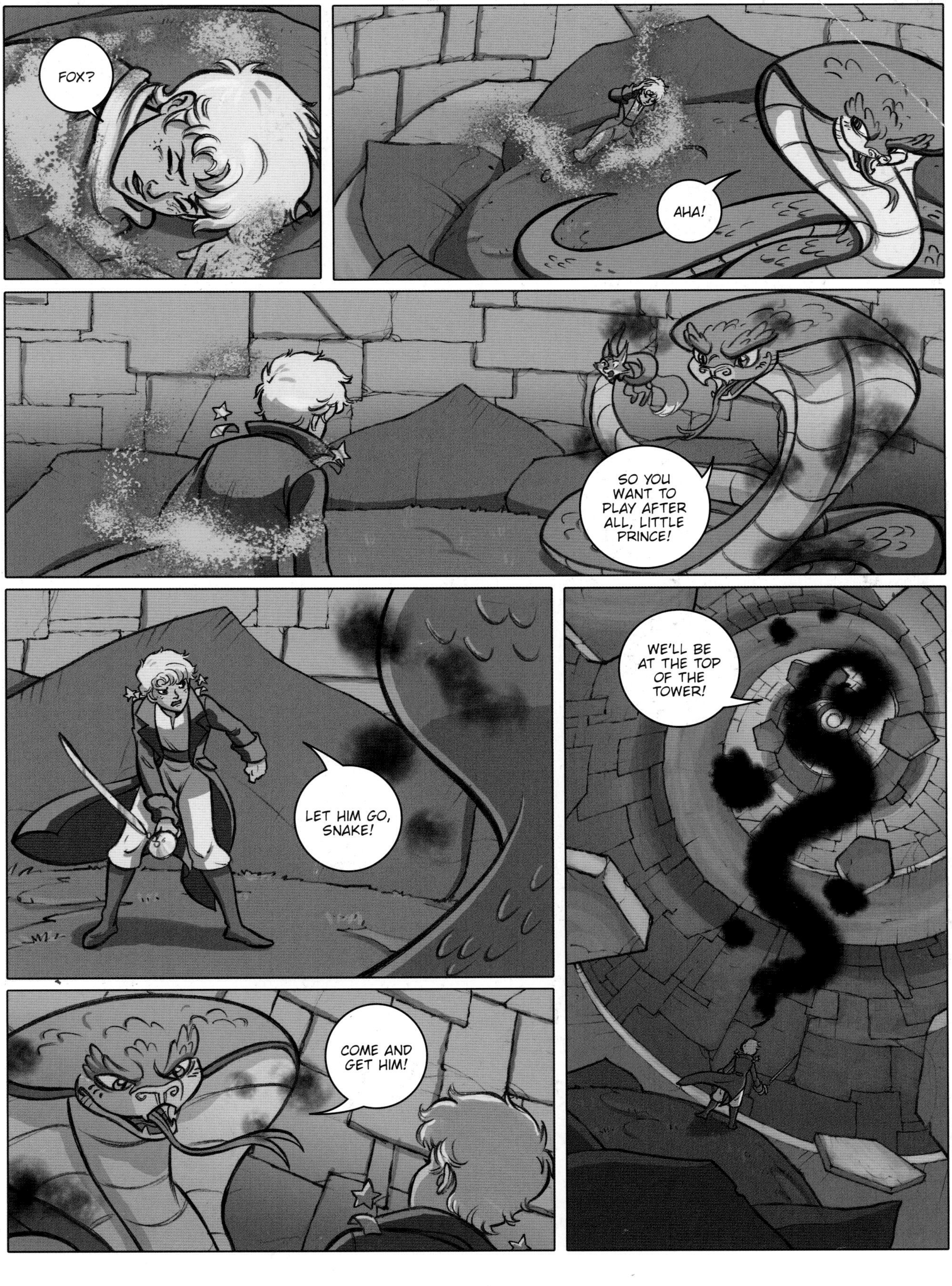
FOX?
AHA!
SO YOU WANT TO PLAY AFTER ALL, LITTLE PRINCE!
LET HIM GO, SNAKE!
COME AND GET HIM!
WE'LL BE AT THE TOP OF THE TOWER!

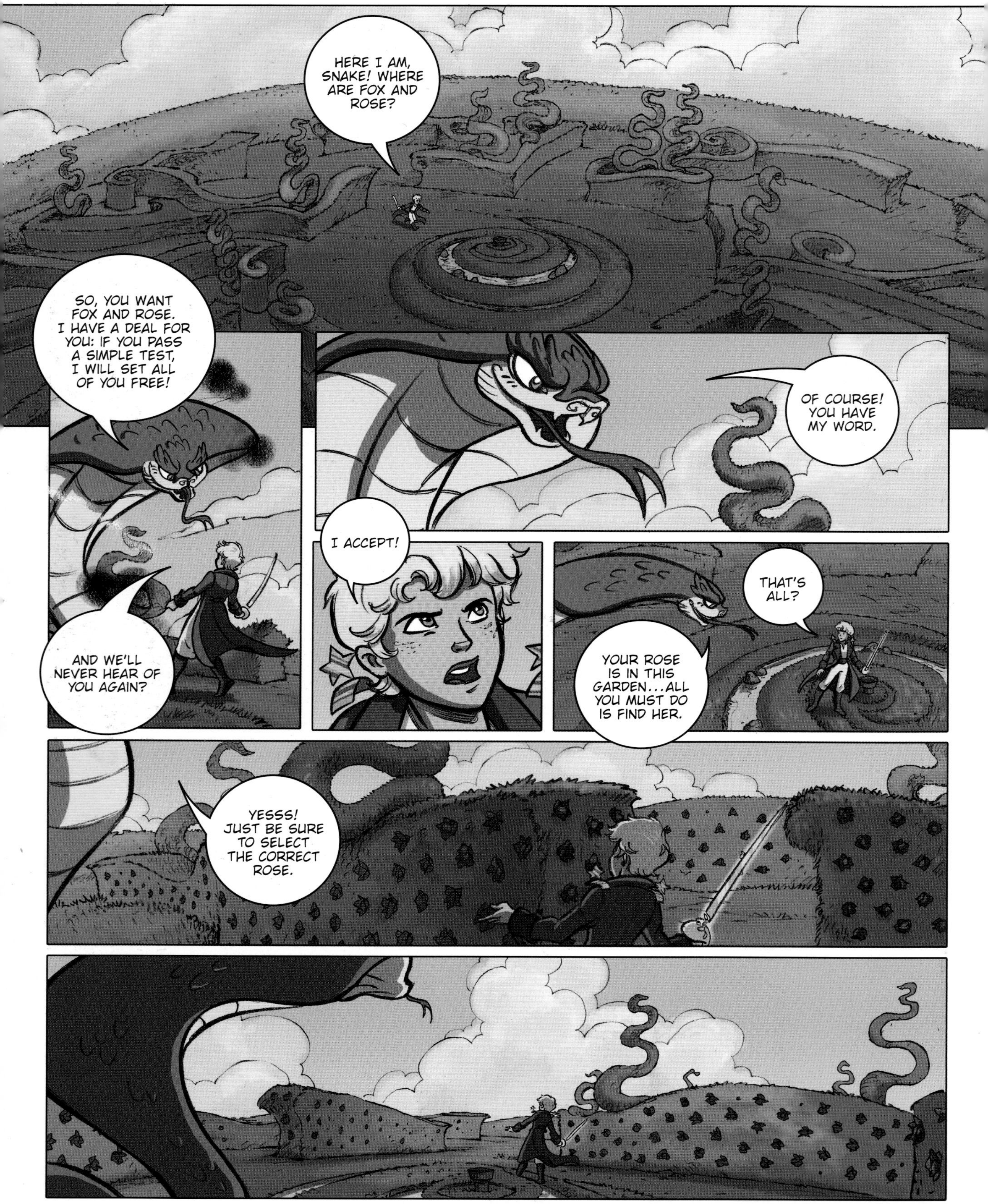
HERE I AM, SNAKE! WHERE ARE FOX AND ROSE?
SO, YOU WANT FOX AND ROSE. I HAVE A DEAL FOR YOU: IF YOU PASS A SIMPLE TEST, I WILL SET ALL OF YOU FREE!
AND WE'LL NEVER HEAR OF YOU AGAIN?
OF COURSE! YOU HAVE MY WORD.
I ACCEPT!
YOUR ROSE IS IN THIS GARDEN...ALL YOU MUST DO IS FIND HER.
THAT'S ALL?
YESSS! JUST BE SURE TO SELECT THE CORRECT ROSE.

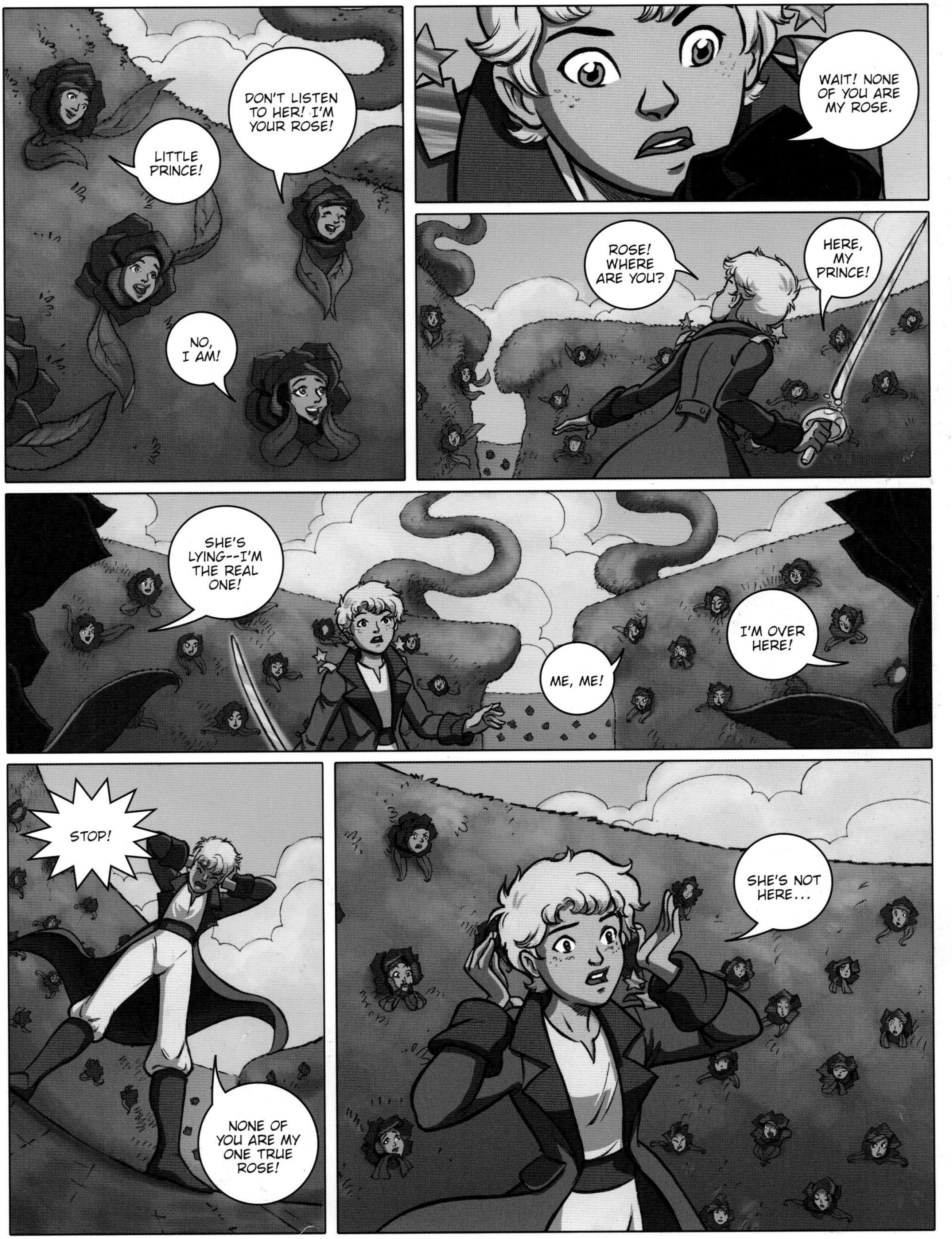
LITTLE PRINCE!
DON'T LISTEN TO HER! I'M YOUR ROSE!
NO, I AM!
WAIT! NONE OF YOU ARE MY ROSE.
ROSE! WHERE ARE YOU?
HERE, MY PRINCE!
SHE'S LYING--I'M THE REAL ONE!
ME, ME!
I'M OVER HERE!
STOP!
NONE OF YOU ARE MY ONE TRUE ROSE!
SHE'S NOT HERE...

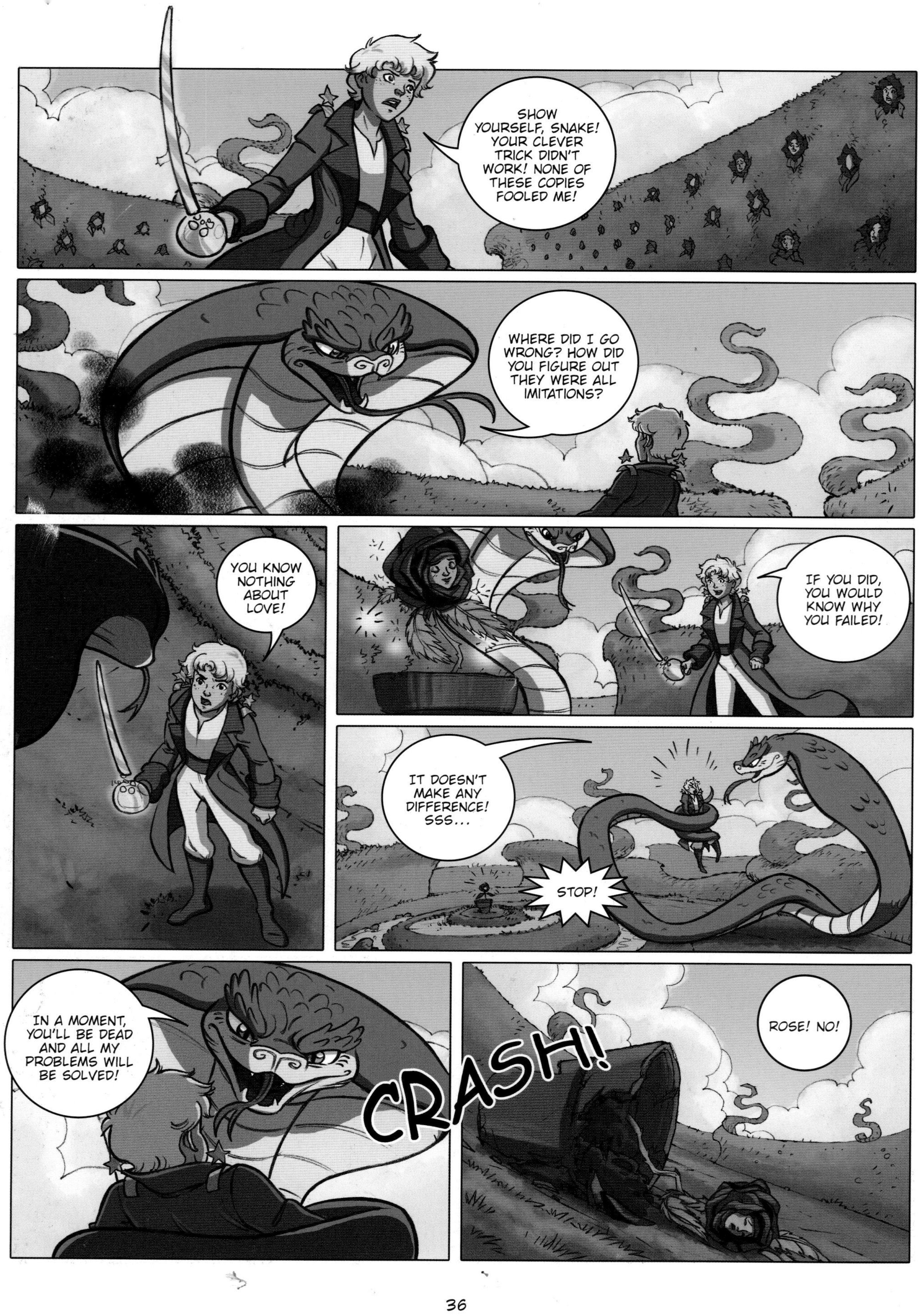
SHOW YOURSELF, SNAKE! YOUR CLEVER TRICK DIDN'T WORK! NONE OF THESE COPIES FOOLED ME!
WHERE DID I GO WRONG? HOW DID YOU FIGURE OUT THEY WERE ALL IMITATIONS?
YOU KNOW NOTHING ABOUT LOVE!
IF YOU DID, YOU WOULD KNOW WHY YOU FAILED!
IT DOESN'T MAKE ANY DIFFERENCE! SSS...
STOP!
IN A MOMENT, YOU'LL BE DEAD AND ALL MY PROBLEMS WILL BE SOLVED!
CRASH!
ROSE! NO!

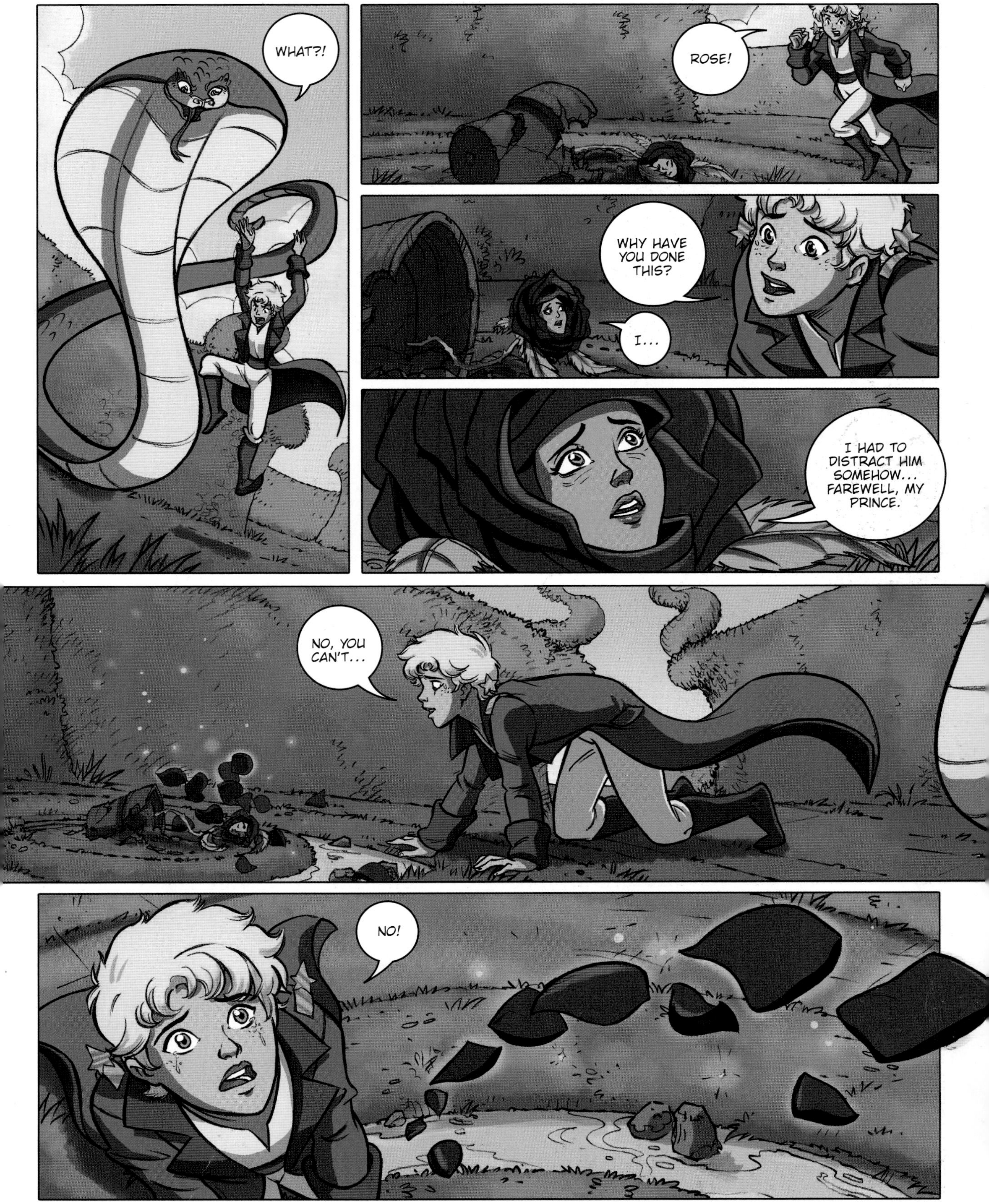
WHAT?!
ROSE!
WHY HAVE YOU DONE THIS?
I...
I HAD TO DISTRACT HIM SOMEHOW... FAREWELL, MY PRINCE.
NO, YOU CAN'T...
NO!

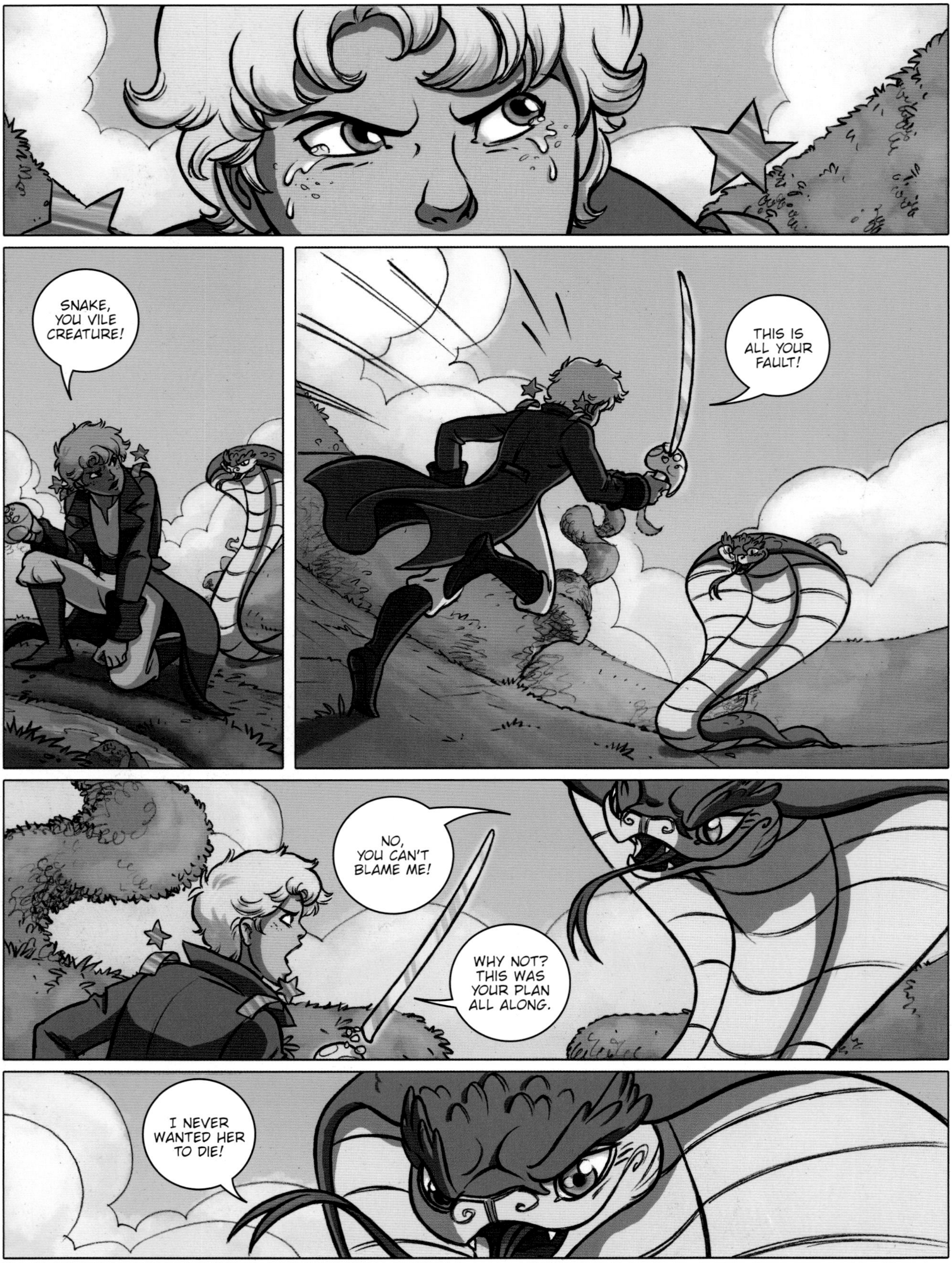
SNAKE, YOU VILE CREATURE!
THIS IS ALL YOUR FAULT!
NO, YOU CAN'T BLAME ME!
WHY NOT? THIS WAS YOUR PLAN ALL ALONG.
I NEVER WANTED HER TO DIE!

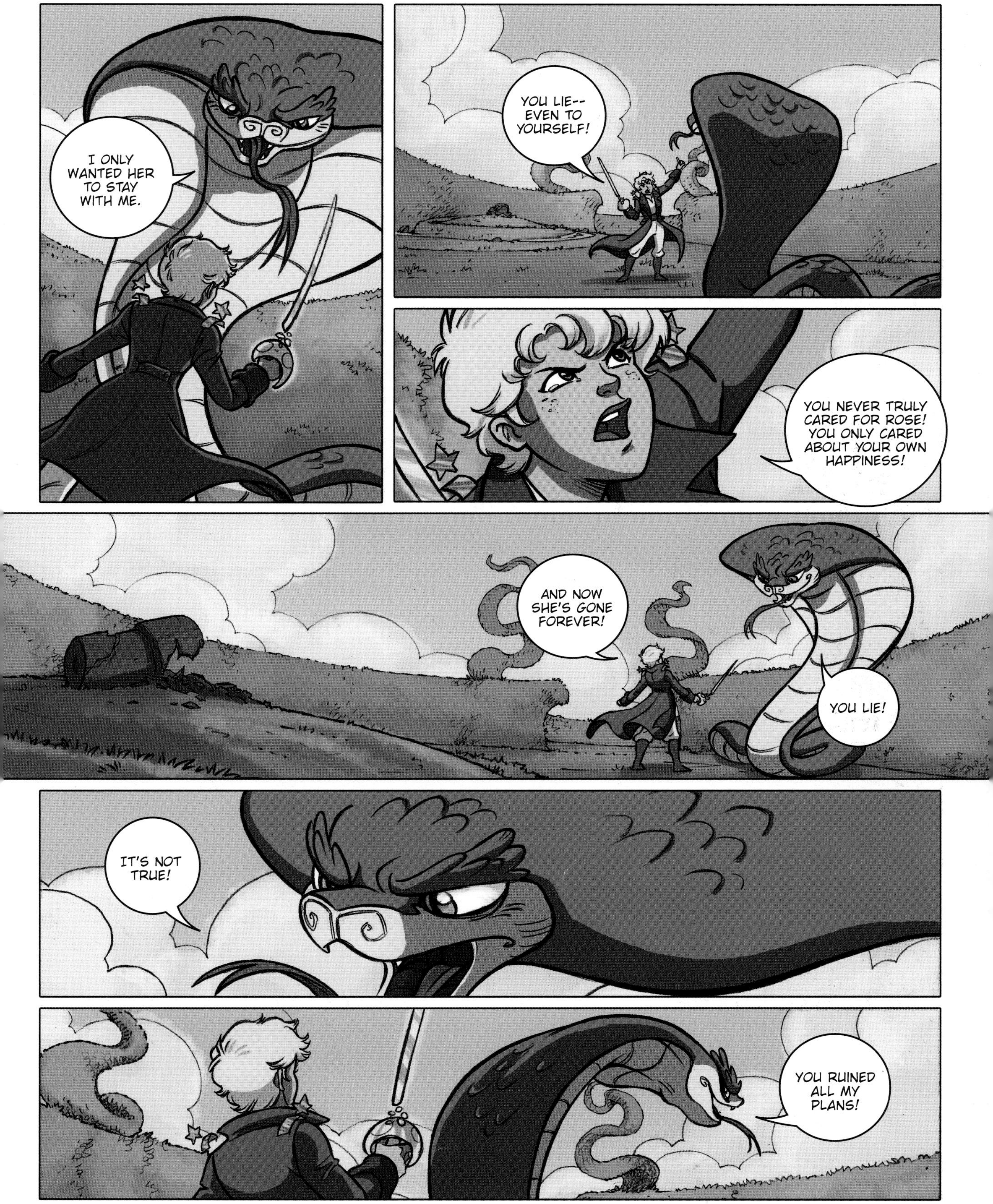
I ONLY WANTED HER TO STAY WITH ME.
YOU LIE-- EVEN TO YOURSELF!
YOU NEVER TRULY CARED FOR ROSE! YOU ONLY CARED ABOUT YOUR OWN HAPPINESS!
AND NOW SHE'S GONE FOREVER!
YOU LIE!
IT'S NOT TRUE!
YOU RUINED ALL MY PLANS!

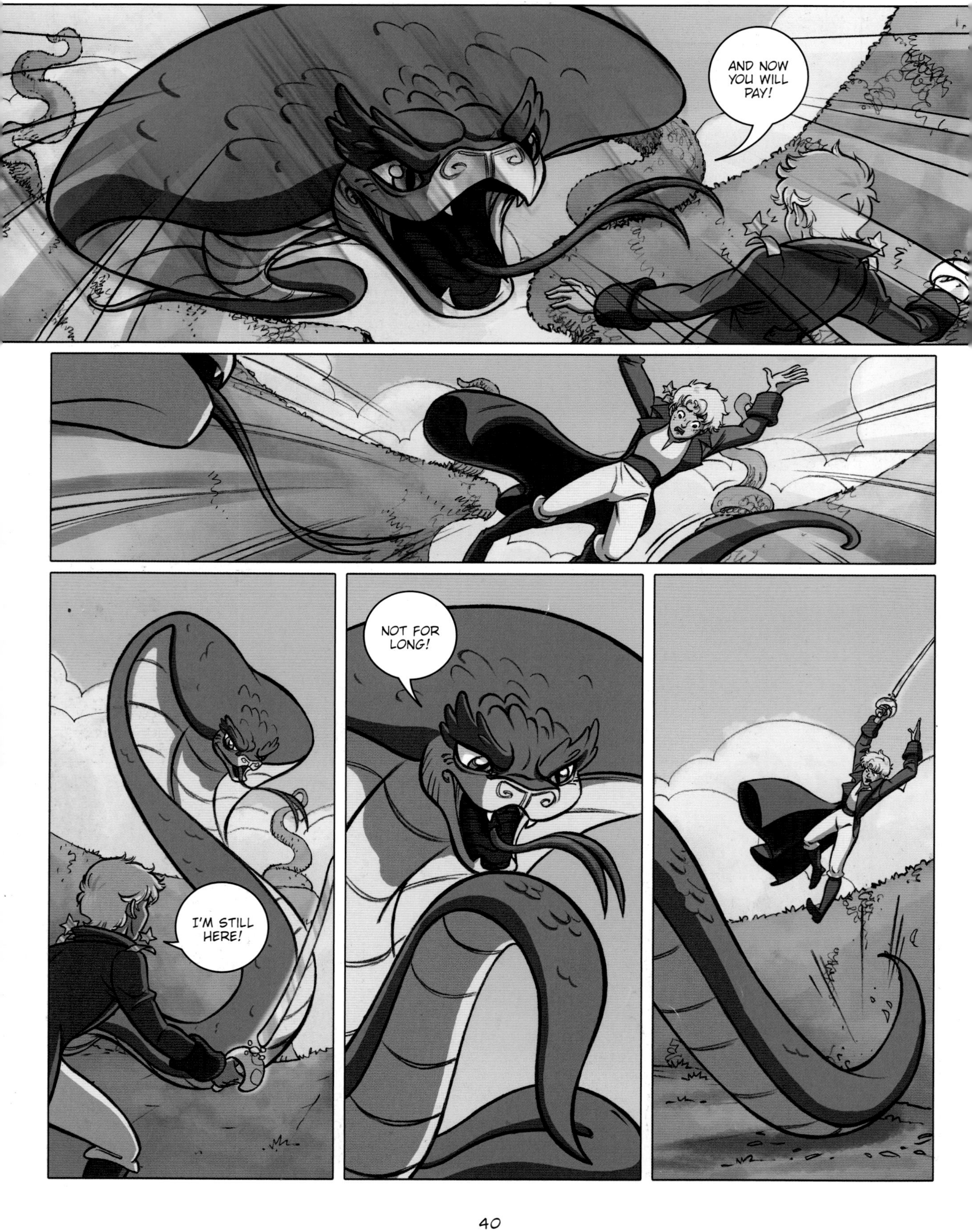
AND NOW YOU WILL PAY!
I'M STILL HERE!
NOT FOR LONG!

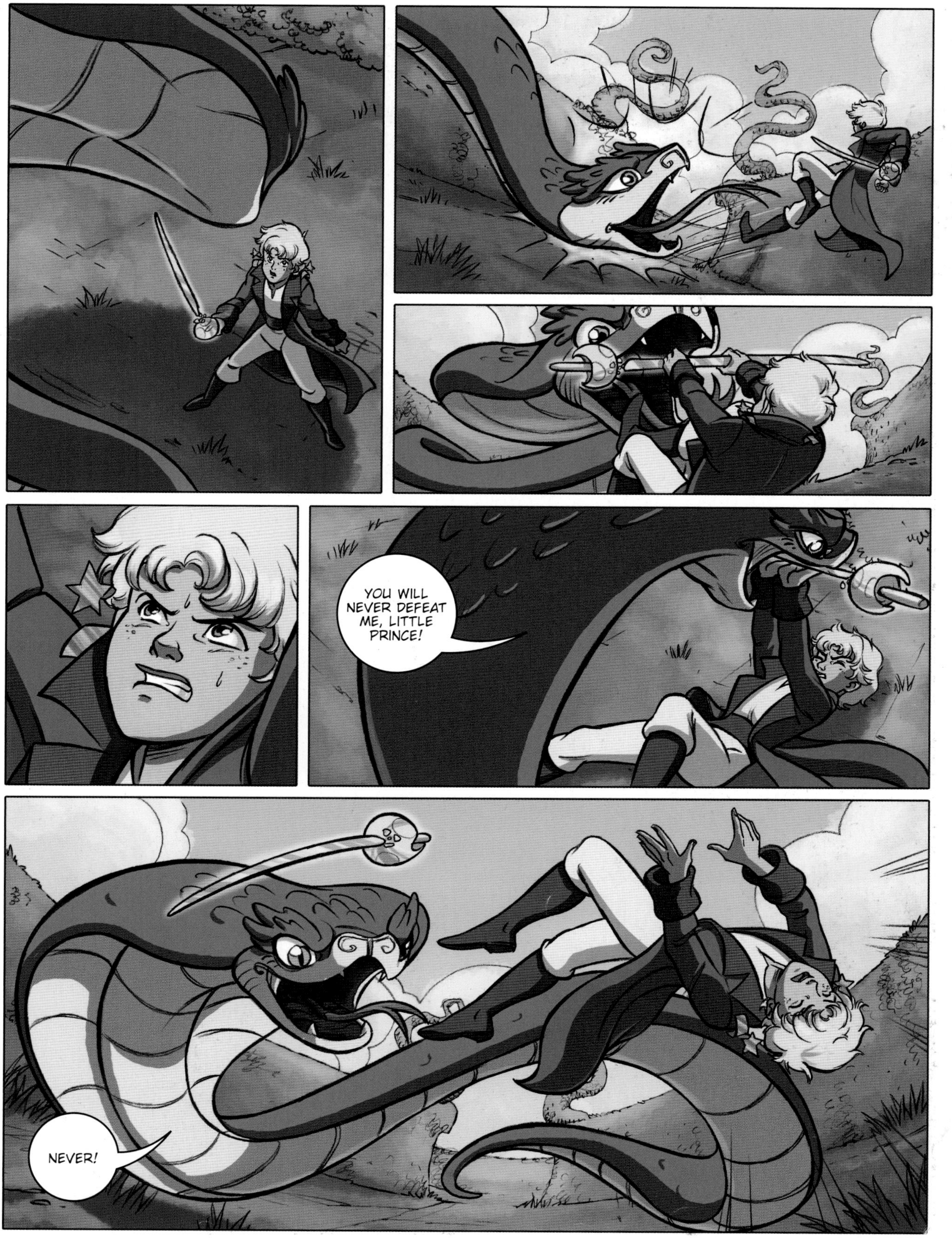
YOU WILL NEVER DEFEAT ME, LITTLE PRINCE!
NEVER!

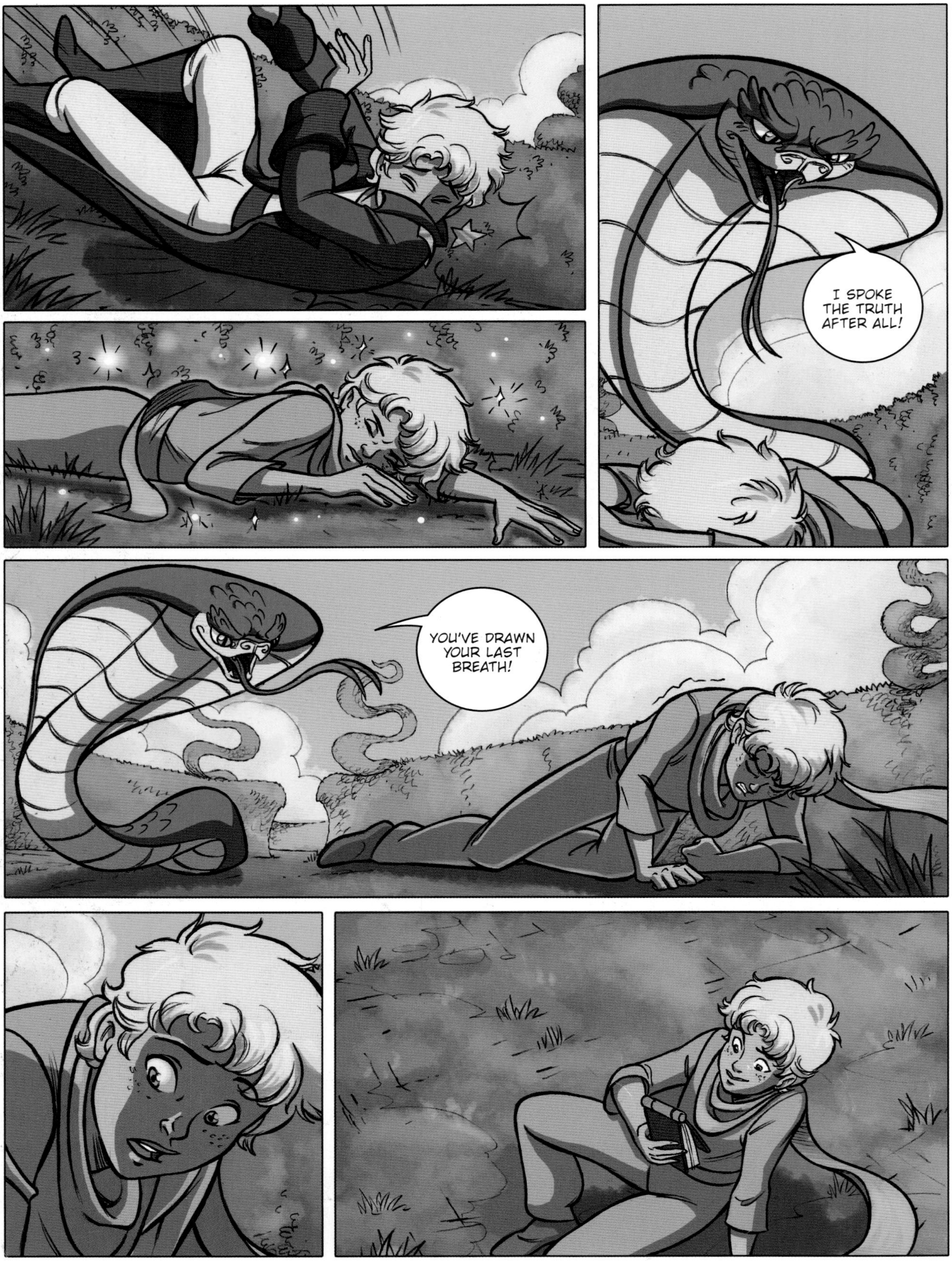
I SPOKE THE TRUTH AFTER ALL!
YOU'VE DRAWN YOUR LAST BREATH!

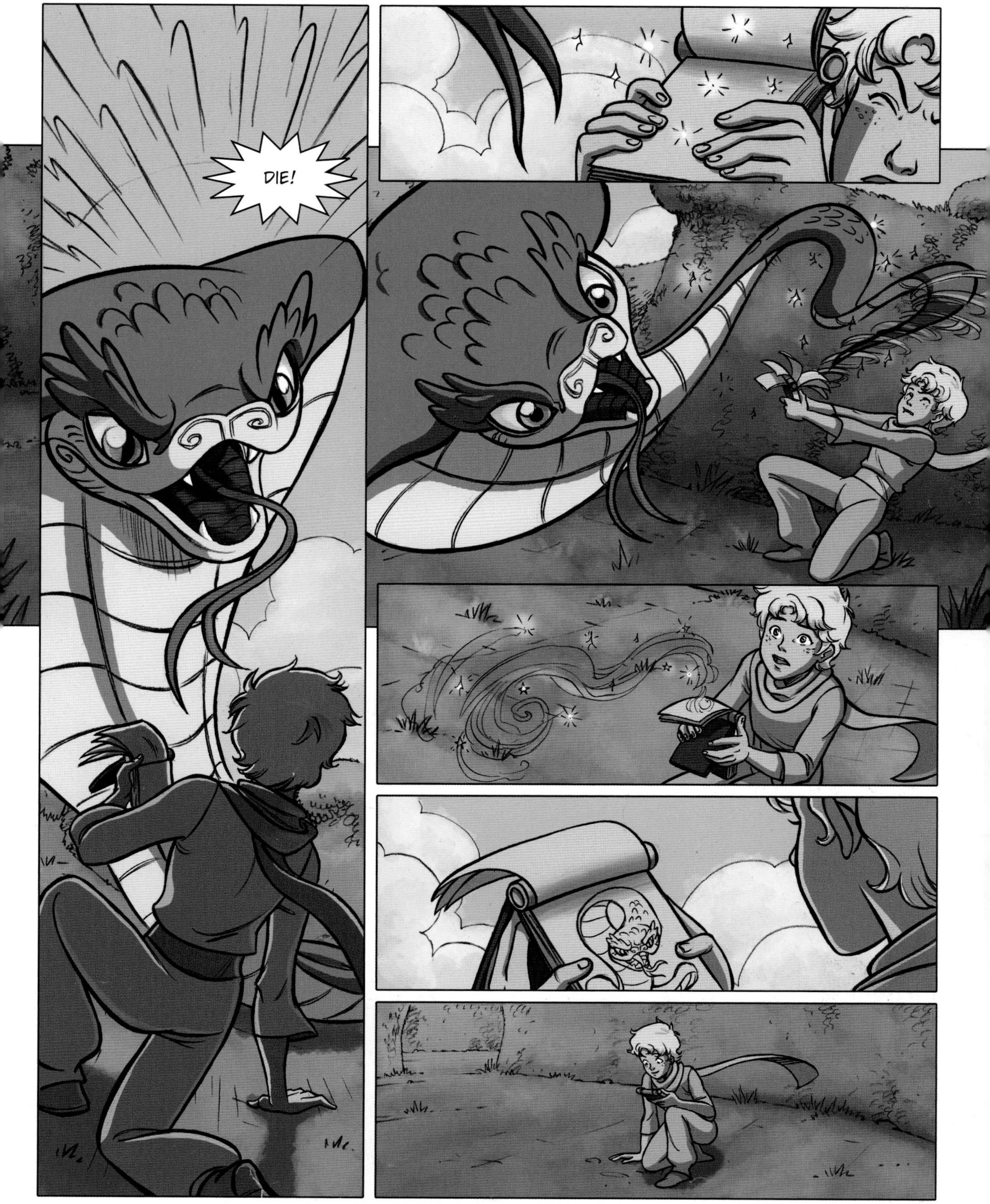
DIE!

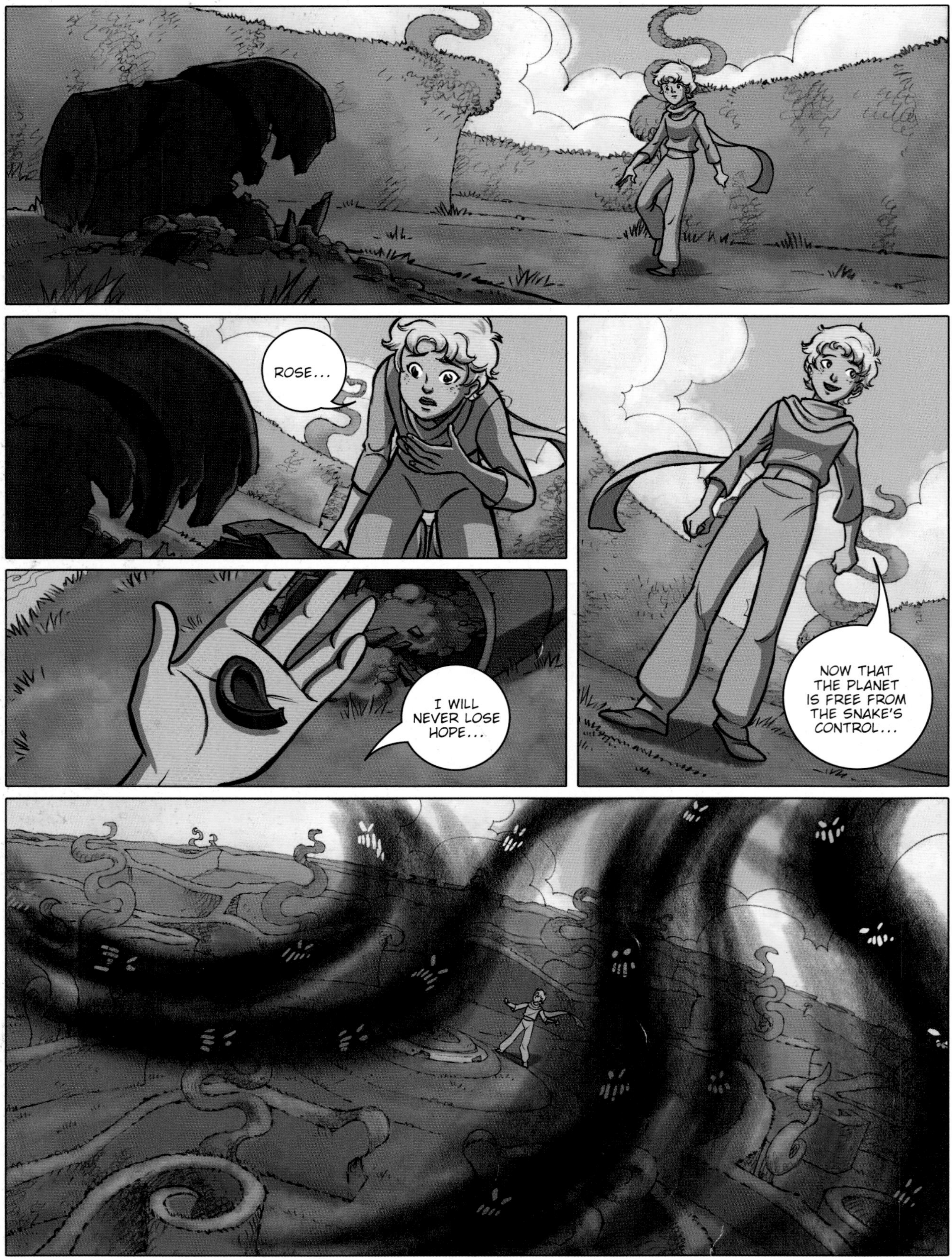
ROSE...
I WILL NEVER LOSE HOPE...
NOW THAT THE PLANET IS FREE FROM THE SNAKE'S CONTROL...

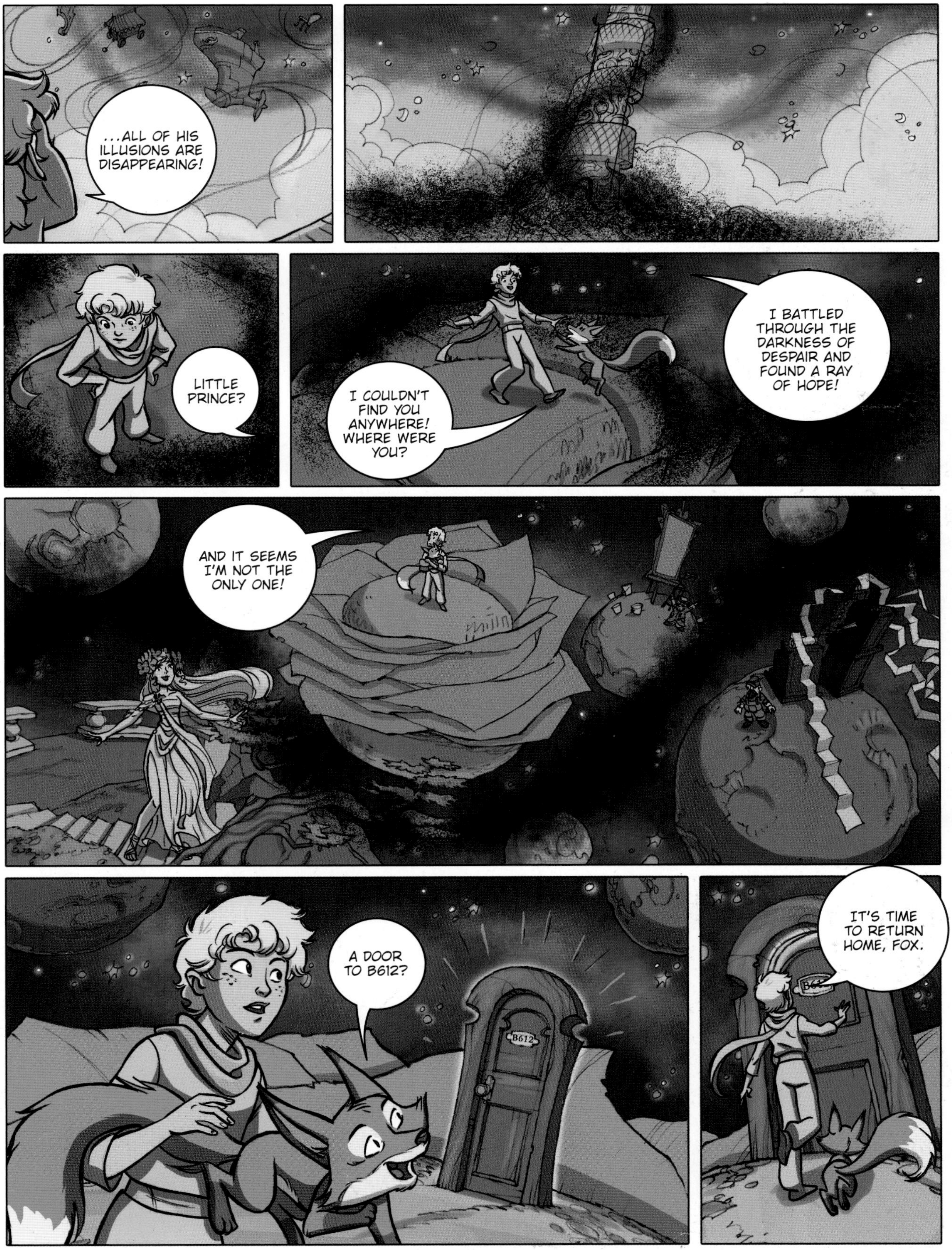
...ALL OF HIS ILLUSIONS ARE DISAPPEARING!
LITTLE PRINCE?
I COULDN'T FIND YOU ANYWHERE! WHERE WERE YOU?
I BATTLED THROUGH THE DARKNESS OF DESPAIR AND FOUND A RAY OF HOPE!
AND IT SEEMS I'M NOT THE ONLY ONE!
A DOOR TO B612?
B612
IT'S TIME TO RETURN HOME, FOX.

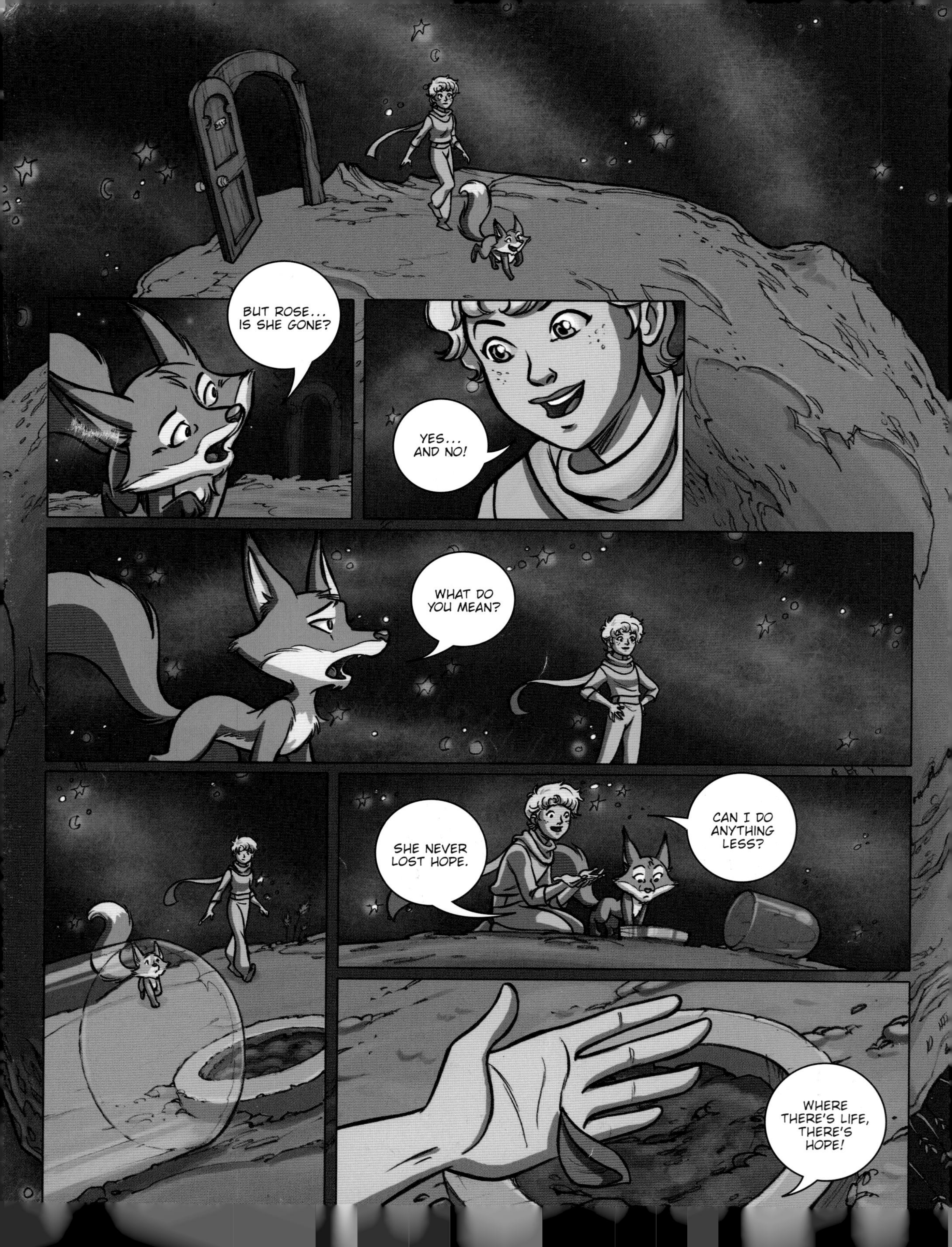

BUT ROSE... IS SHE GONE?
YES... AND NO!
WHAT DO YOU MEAN?
SHE NEVER LOST HOPE.
CAN I DO ANYTHING LESS?
WHERE THERE'S LIFE, THERE'S HOPE!

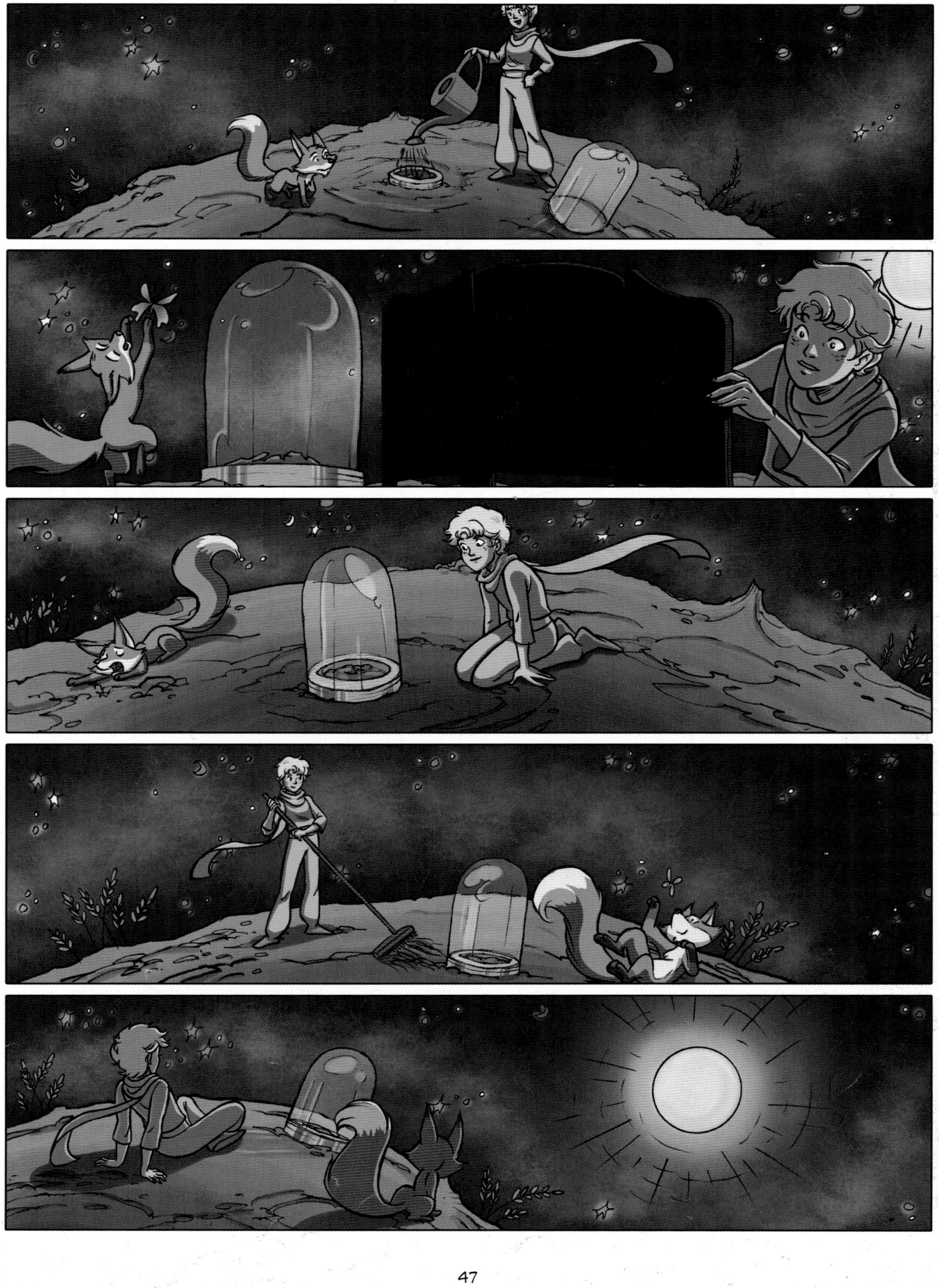

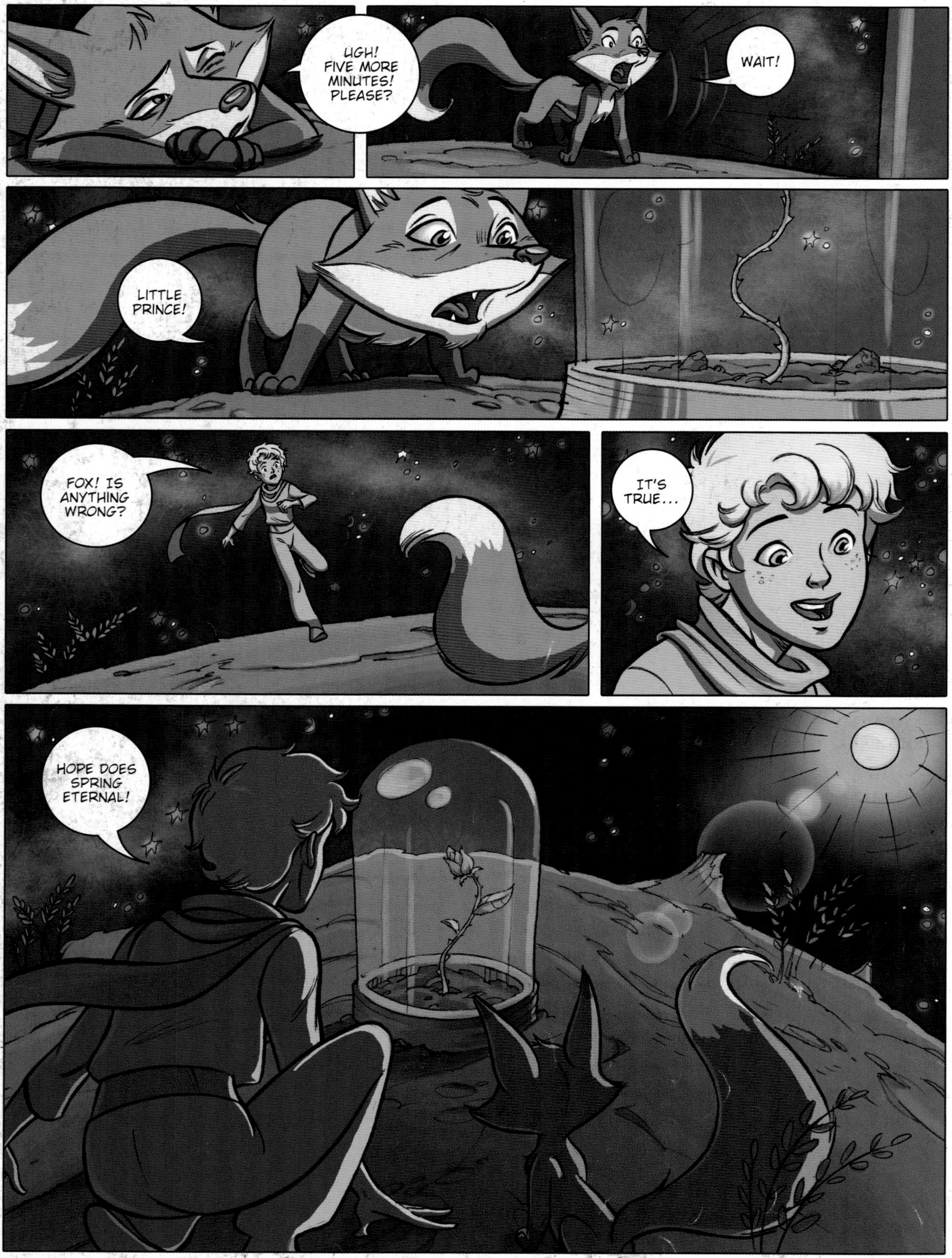
UGH! FIVE MORE MINUTES! PLEASE?
WAIT!
LITTLE PRINCE!
FOX! IS ANYTHING WRONG?
IT'S TRUE...
HOPE DOES SPRING ETERNAL!

Read all the Books in *The Little Prince* series

Book 1: The Planet of Wind
Book 2: The Planet of the Firebird
Book 3: The Planet of Music
Book 4: The Planet of Jade
Book 5: The Star Snatcher's Planet
Book 6: The Planet of the Night Globes
Book 7: The Planet of the Overhearers
Book 8: The Planet of the Tortoise Driver
Book 9: The Planet of the Giant
Book 10: The Planet of Trainiacs
Book 11: The Planet of Libris
Book 12: The Planet of Ludokaa
Book 13: The Planet of Tear-Eaters
Book 14: The Planet of the Grand Buffoon
Book 15: The Planet of the Gargand
Book 16: The Planet of Gehom
Book 17: The Planet of the Bubble Gob
Book 18: The Planet of Time
Book 19: The Planet of the Cublix
Book 20: The Planet of Coppelius
Book 21: The Planet of Okidians
Book 22: The Planet of Ashkabaar
Book 23: The Planet of Bamalias
Book 24: The Planet of the Snake

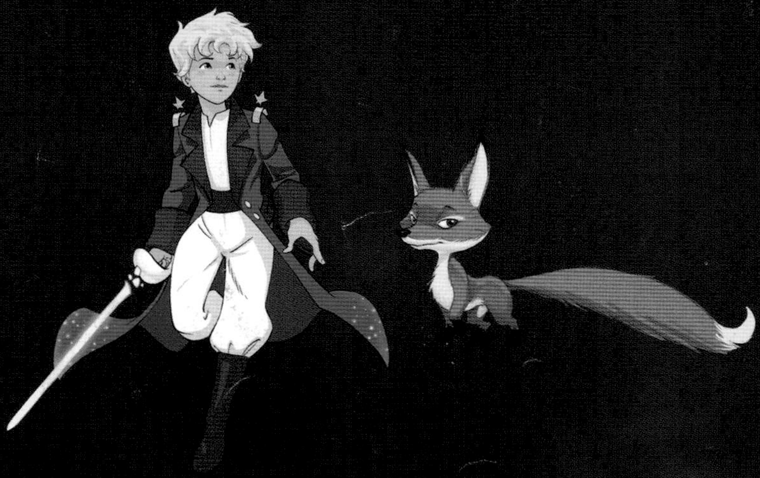

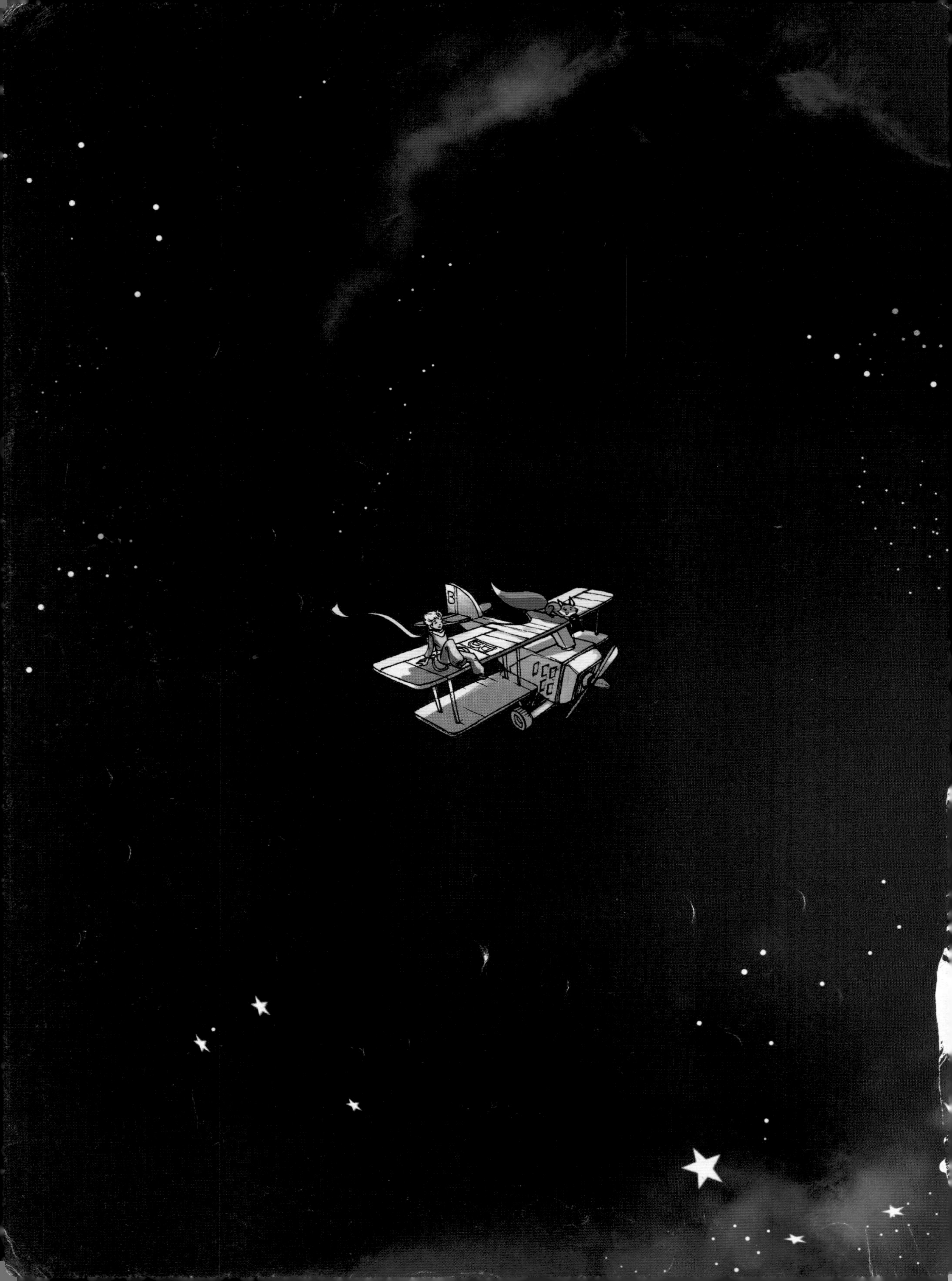

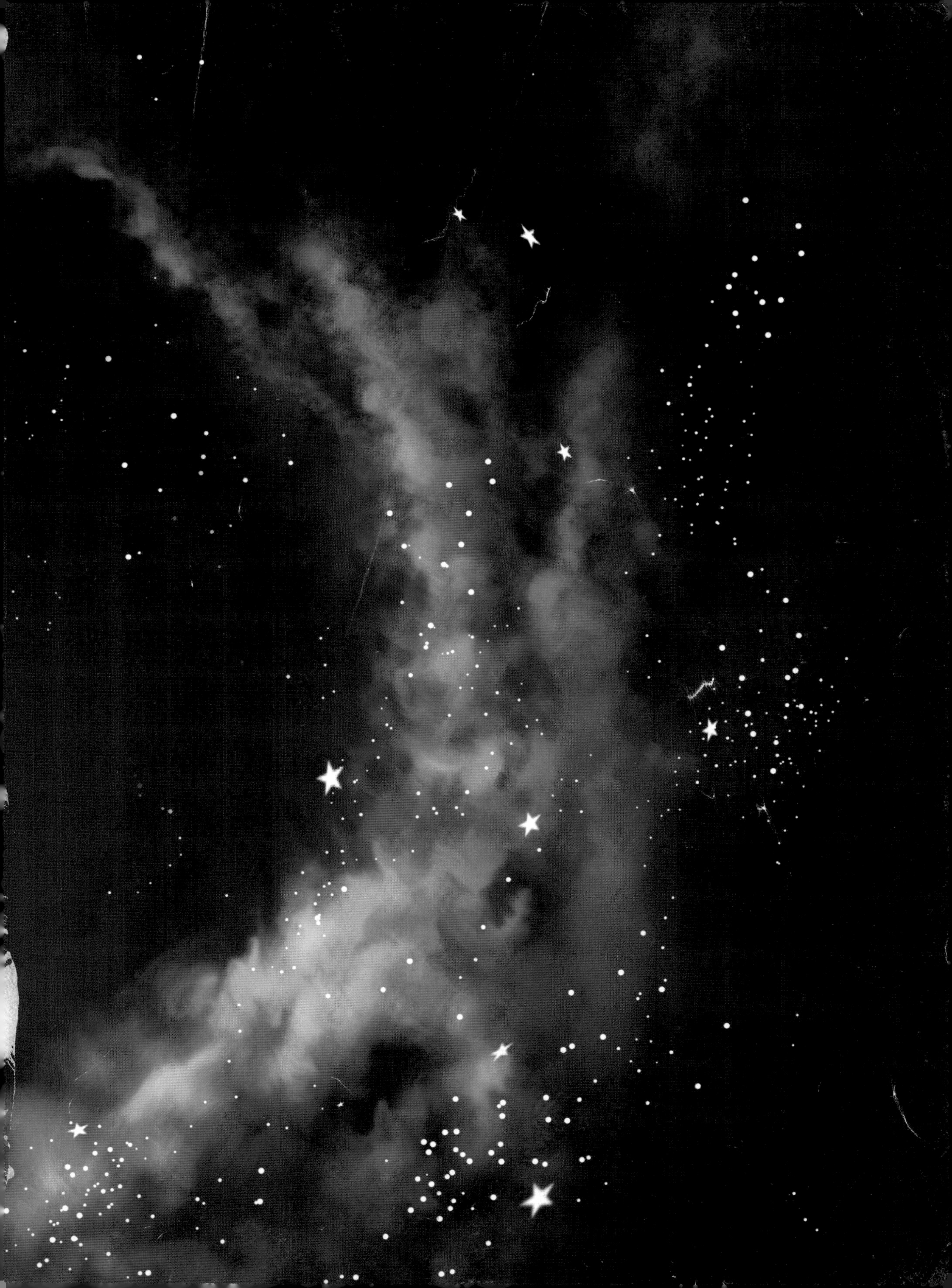